A SPARK IN DARKNESS

LORANA HOOPES

This book is dedicated to my readers, especially those who took a chance on the first book The Still Small Voice and encouraged me to continue the story. Also to my gym family - you have always been there to push and encourage me. Special thanks to Julien, Jason, Jon, Jonathon, Israel, Molly, and Kris who push me to work hard even when I'm tired.

I know that none of us have a perfect idea of what will happen after the rapture or if there even is a rapture, but I grew up believing there was and that believers will be taken before the tribulation begins. Even if you don't believe the same as I do, I hope you will find God's work throughout this book. It took me over a year to write the sequel because I wanted to do it right.

I will warn you that while this book has an ending, you will still be left with questions. I promise to answer them soon as I have at least one more book if not two planned in the series. So thank you for joining me and I hope you'll stay for the entire ride.

NOTE FROM THE AUTHOR

Because it's been so long since I wrote The Still Small Voice, I thought I would give you a brief rundown of that book and who the main characters in this book are. If you've already read it, you can skip this section.

Dr. Kat Jameson - oncologist. Her best friend Stella O'Donnell died in The Still Small Voice, leaving Kat to deal with her anger. Soon, Kat began seeing lights around people. She has no idea what to think until Jordan Wright shows up on her doorstep and tells her she has a gift.

Jordan Wright - young, college-aged student who was drugged and raped at a frat party. After giving her baby up for adoption, she asks God to use her and begins receiving visions. Her visions lead her from Texas to Washington where she finds Kat. (You can find more of Jordan's story in When Hearts Collide)

Patrick O'Donnell - husband of Stella (deceased) and father to Maddie. He has stepped in as a friend to Kat.

Micah Gibson - associate of Kat's in the first book who reveals he is an angel at the end. Tells her that the lights she is seeing are angels protecting people who are considering turning to God. Tells her to find Raven Ryder.

Raven Ryder - Feisty, kick boxer who doesn't like Kat and doesn't believe in God. Abused in her past which has created her hardened exterior.

Jason - kickboxing trainer at the gym. He likes Kat, but she doesn't want to date him knowing her time is short. Raven is pursuing him, but so far he hasn't shown interest beyond friendship.

Brian - owner of the gym.

Other gym members mentioned - Jon and Lilly

The Still Small Voice ends with Kat being told she needs to find Raven and her telling Jordan that Micah said they had a job to do. She invites Jordan to move in with her for however long is necessary.

This book picks up a few days later.

MONDAY AFTERNOON

The sound of chaos assaulted Raven Ryder as she stepped out of the gym. A car horn emitted a continuous blaring as if something or perhaps someone was lodged against it. Black smoke filled the air from the three accidents she could see up and down College Street. Who knew how many more there were across the city? Across the state? Would there even be enough ambulances to attend to them all? Would there be enough doctors?

It was the middle of summer, yet the air felt cold. So cold. Raven had no idea what this new reality might mean, but she did understand that life as she had known it was about to change radically.

"Did you see where they went?" A hand touched her arm, but the eyes of the woman were blank, overcome with fear and disbelief. Blood flowed from an open wound on her head, but she seemed oblivious to it. She hadn't even bothered to wipe it away. "I can't find Amelia anywhere."

"They're gone," Raven said, shaking the woman's hand from her arm as if her very touch might transfer the disease of confusion. She may not know what the next seven years held, but she knew what her next step was. Kat's house. Somewhere in Kat's house was a document that Raven needed. A document that would guide her and possibly save her life over the next few years.

"Gone? They couldn't be gone. Something took them. Maybe aliens. Aliens could take them all at once, right?"

"Yeah, maybe." Raven walked away from the woman, but others were beginning to wander her way. People who had been in the cars that now littered the street. People from nearby businesses. They all appeared as dazed as the woman behind her - like zombies. Raven had to get away from them, but would the streets even be driveable? It was a cluttered mess here, would there be room to maneuver? Kat's house wasn't far, but Raven wanted the safety of her Jeep around her.

"Raven, where are you going?" Jason stood a few feet from the entrance to the gym, a purple bruise already forming on the side of his face. He was an amazing trainer and fast as lightning, but he'd obviously hit something. "Brian's called an ambulance and the police. He wants everyone to stay put until this gets sorted out."

Brian was the owner of the gym, and normally Raven would follow what he said, but this time she shook her head. There was no use staying here. The police wouldn't be able to help. "I have to get to Kat's house. She left me something that explains all this. Something I'm going to need." She turned back to assess her options. The main entrance to the gym parking lot was not an option. People blocked it and an accident filled all four lanes of College Street less than a block from the exit. Perhaps the back entrance would be passable. That street was less heavily trafficked. She might get lucky enough to weave through whatever cars might be there.

"Need? For what? Right now we need to find the kids and Kat. Where is Kat anyway?" His eyes wandered to Kat's blue Mini Cooper still parked in the space nearest the side door.

She turned back to him, intensity in her eyes. "Kat is gone, Jason. The kids are gone. We could search forever, but we'll never find them."

"Gone? Gone where?"

"Come with me. I'll show you and it will all make sense." Raven motioned for him to follow her, but he seemed unsure. His gaze flicked back to the gym door. "You can stay if you want, but no answers reside in there. I can give you answers if you come with me."

His curiosity won out as she figured it would, and he followed her to the Jeep. After they were both buckled in, she fired up the engine and the radio blasted forth the emergency broadcast warning.

"This is an emergency alert. People are being encouraged to stay inside their houses. At least five planes have fallen from the sky over Washington state leaving fires and catastrophes in their wake."

"Wait, planes are falling from the sky?" Jason turned his attention to the sky out the window. "How is that even possible? Was this a terrorist attack?"

Raven knew he was probably thinking back to September 11th, the worst terrorist attack in US history. Planes had appeared to fall out of the sky then, but only four. And they'd been hijacked. These planes hadn't, and if five had fallen over Washington state alone, how many others had fallen across the world? She put her finger to her lips to shush him and turned the radio up.

"In addition, reports of car accidents are flooding in faster than ambulances can be dispatched. 911 is overloaded with calls and is asking that if your situation is not a life threatening emergency that you please try later. The police are setting up a hotline for all missing persons, but it is not online yet. Please hold missing person calls until the hotline has been established."

Jason blinked and ran a hand across his stubbled chin. "So, this isn't just here? It didn't just affect the gym?"

Raven sighed. "No, this affected the world, and those missing people aren't coming back."

"How do you know?"

Raven looked behind her before throwing the Jeep in reverse and backing out. "Because Kat told me just like she told you. These people are gone because they were raptured, and now I have a job to do."

He gripped the dashboard as she threw the Jeep into drive and gunned it. "Job? What job?"

But Raven didn't answer. She didn't know the answer. She only had the few pieces that Kat had been able to tell her. The truth was she didn't really know what the future held.

❦ 2 ❦

ONE WEEK EARLIER - SATURDAY

An angel. Micah Gibson was an angel, and Kat had a job to do. Kat Jameson stared at the open Bible in front of her and sighed. She should have asked more questions, gotten a road map of how exactly she was supposed to connect with the one girl at the gym who seemed to loathe her. But how did you think to ask questions when the guy you'd thought was just a normal peer spread his celestial wings in your office and told you he was an angel? How did you think beyond the present when he told you the lights you'd been seeing were angels protecting people and that it was your job to witness to them? To save them.

Kat still had no idea why she'd been chosen. She had claimed to be a Christian since high school when she'd given her heart to God at a service, but she'd certainly had her ups and downs on the journey. She'd pushed God to the side while she went through college and medical school. Sure, she'd attended a church service every couple of weeks but not because she wanted to. Not because she had a burning desire to be in the presence of the Lord. No, she'd gone because Stella had asked her to. Stella had been the rock, the anchor, the one on fire for God. But now Stella was gone. And even after that, Kat couldn't say she was great at remembering to read the Bible every day. Now, she wished she had been.

Micah had said the end was coming soon. The Rapture. The Tribulation. And it was her job to tell as many people as possible about God. To *save* as many people as possible. But she wasn't even sure what that meant. People had been talking about The Rapture for years, but no one knew much about it. Even the Book of Revelation, which was supposed to give the most information on it, was incredibly hard to decipher. Was it literal? Metaphorical? Even the so called "experts" she was Googling couldn't seem to agree. So how was she, a run of the mill oncologist, supposed to have all the answers?

Heaving another sigh, she pushed back from the table and put a kettle of water on the stove. Maybe tea would help clear her head. Tea always seemed to help - ease worries, relax her soul. Her mind wandered back through the years to the many times she and Stella had chatted over tea - the day Stella told her she was getting married, the day she'd said she was pregnant. It seemed that big discussions always happened over tea. How she wished Stella was here now to help her figure out what to do.

Footsteps in the hallway drew her attention to the entrance that connected the kitchen to the rest of the house. A moment later, Jordan's blonde head appeared in the doorway. A few days ago, Jordan Wright had been a stranger. A young college-aged kid who'd traveled across the country to tell Kat that she'd seen her in a vision and God had a plan for her. Kat had thought she was crazy at first, but Jordan had known about the lights. She'd shared her own visions with Kat - seeing her yelling at the sky, collapsed and crying under the window after Stella's death - things she could not have known which made it harder to dismiss her. Then her mother had told her she spoke to Jesus as a young child, and Micah had revealed he was an angel. Suddenly, Jordan's story hadn't sounded so far-fetched. Not that Kat went around asking, but she didn't know anyone else who'd ever seen a real angel.

So, Kat had offered Jordan a place to stay as long as she needed. She wasn't Stella for sure - no one would replace her best friend - but she was rather like the younger sister Kat had never had.

"You making tea?" Jordan asked as she crossed to the table and dropped into the chair opposite Kat. She was already in her pajamas - checkered flannel pants and an oversized t-shirt that said "Tea Trails Begin Here" but she didn't look ready for bed. Tiny lines spread out from around her eyes as if something was bothering her. Of course it could just be the bombshell that Kat had dropped on her yesterday. Micah had said that Jordan was a part of this job Kat had to do, and she took it to mean that Jordan might not return to Texas before the rapture. Leaving for a visit and realizing you might never return home would certainly stress her out.

"You want some?" Kat opened the cupboard and pulled out two mugs, but the question was more out of habit than curiosity. The girl's shirt declared her love for tea.

"Please."

"Did you get settled okay?" Kat leaned against the gold-flecked marble counter as she waited for the whistle to sound. She'd set Jordan up in her guest room which was cozy though decorated simply, but that wasn't what she was asking Jordan. Not really, anyway. She wanted to make sure the girl was as comfortable as she could be, especially since Kat was little more than a stranger.

Jordan's thin shoulders rose in a defeated shrug. "Yeah, I guess. I didn't bring much. Though I didn't know how long I'd be gone, I packed light. Most of my stuff is in a storage place back in Texas. It's kind of hard realizing I may never see it again or need it."

Kat could relate. Though she hadn't had to leave her home, there were things that had been weighing on her since Micah revealed himself. Mainly all the things she had yet to do. "I know. People always say that seeing Jesus is what we should want most in the world, but I have to tell you that I'm scared. I haven't done everything I wanted to yet." Of course, Micah hadn't told her how long they still had. She didn't know if he even knew the exact time. Maybe it was years, but she doubted it. If he had revealed himself to her, the time had to be coming soon.

A tight smile formed on Jordan's lips. "Yeah, I know. I'm so young, and even though I know I'm doing God's work, I still have regrets."

The kettle whistled and Kat poured the water into the two oversized mugs before carrying them to the table.

"Anyway." Jordan blew the word out with a sigh. "How about you? Find anything that will help us navigate this?"

Kat looked down at the open Bible. "Not much. I'm trying to decipher Revelation, but I'm no Biblical scholar, and even those who are, don't always agree. I can't tell if these churches John mentions were only churches back then or if what we are seeing today falls under them too. I mean some things certainly fit. He says the church of Ephesus hates evil, but they've forgotten their first love. I assume that means they've become legalistic and forgotten Jesus. We certainly see that in some who claim to be Christian.

"Then there's Smyrna, which is about people who claim to be believers but aren't. I'm sure we will see many of them. The church of Pergamum is a little harder to decipher. John says they live in the shadow of Satan's throne but still follow Jesus."

"Missionaries maybe?" Jordan asked as she lifted her mug and blew lightly into it. "Or people who work in less than ideal situations hoping to share the gospel?"

Kat pursed her lips. "I don't know because then he says they indulge the Balaam crowd and put up with the Nicolaitans."

"I'm not super familiar with Balaam. Have you found anything about him?"

"Yeah." Kat flipped back in her Bible to the book of Numbers. "He was once a strong prophet of God. He was offered wealth to curse the Israelites, but he said he couldn't go against what God said to him. So, he ended up blessing them instead."

Confusion marred Jordan's face. "I don't understand then. Why wouldn't we want to be like Balaam?"

Kat picked up her own mug and let the warmth roll down her arms. "Because, evidently, he later found a way to get his wealth without cursing Israel directly. Peter says he enticed them to sin through idols and sexual immorality."

"So, these people might be those who consider themselves believers but worship idols or engage in immoral behavior?"

Kat nodded and took a sip of her tea while she considered her answer. "Maybe. We certainly see that today with people treating their electronics like idols and sex like holding hands."

Jordan chuffed and turned her mug in a slow circle on the table. "Yeah, you should have seen college. Even in Texas where it's still fairly conservative, I knew plenty of girls who slept with every guy they dated." She dropped her eyes to her mug and her voice grew quiet. "Don't get me started on frat parties."

Kat knew Jordan was thinking about her own encounter. She had been drugged and raped at a frat party, and while Kat knew Jordan hadn't wanted to be raped, she had been looking to hook up that night. Sexual immorality was prevalent all over college campuses. It had been even years ago when Kat had attended, and it appeared worse now. "It's rampant everywhere. How could it not be? It's pervasive in our movies and TV. Virgins are labeled as stupid or losers. I try to stay out of hospital gossip, but I've heard enough to know that it goes on there as well. You couldn't pay me enough to sleep in an on-call room unless it was disinfected thoroughly first."

She shuddered as she thought of all the hospital employees she had heard used the on-call rooms as quick hook up places. Of course they were only rumors; she'd never seen a quickie happening, but that many rumors couldn't all be wrong. "So, maybe the people who represent Pergamum are believers who refrain from evil but permit people around them to commit sexual sins."

Jordan sighed and tucked a strand of hair behind her ear. "Sadly, I think there's a lot of that in churches right now. I'm not for fire and brimstone, but I wish they would stop preaching that anything goes. This whole 'if it makes you happy mentality' definitely goes against God's teaching, and I think it's led many good Christians astray." She paused as if thinking back over her own life choices. Then she cleared her throat and met Kat's gaze again. "What about the Nicolaitans? Who are they?"

Frustration coursed through Kat as she flipped back to Revelation. "I don't know. There's even fewer mentions of them. Some believe there was a man named Nicolas who was once a deacon but then followed Balaam's path and encouraged people to sin by eating unholy food and committing sexual sins. Others believe that they weren't called from any one man but from the Greek word 'Nicolah' which means 'let us eat.' Of course, The *Left Behind* series even stated that a man named Nicolai was the anti-Christ, so regardless of who they are, their actions grieve God, but I don't know what we're supposed to do with this information. I wish Micah had given me more of a hint of how to do this."

"Maybe it's not about the details," Jordan said.

Kat's brows edged together, furrowing her brow. "What do you mean?"

"I mean I get visions of people and what they need to hear. Does it matter if they represent Ephesus or Pergamum? You see lights of people being protected by angels - people you're supposed to witness to. Maybe the details don't matter, and we need to just focus on that."

A piece of Kat knew Jordan was right. She was focusing on the details partly because all of this was overwhelming, but there was a piece of her that knew the details might be important. Raven didn't seem like the type of girl to become a believer simply because Kat told her she needed to. No, she seemed like the kind who would need facts. The kind who would need to be told what would happen and then see it come true. And that's why Kat needed more information. She wanted to give Raven clear signs to look for. But she couldn't do it alone. She would have to find someone else who could clarify things for her.

Jordan lay in the unfamiliar bed that night and tried to keep her tears at bay. They stung the back of her eyes in their effort to escape. It wasn't that she had left that much back in Texas - a few friends, her overbearing mother, the son whom she'd given up for adoption - no, it was exactly what she'd told Kat tonight. She was feeling regret, and, if she were honest, a little anger. Why did the rapture have to come now? Before she'd really gotten to live life?

Yes, she knew the Bible talked about how much better it would be in Heaven, and she believed it, but she'd never be able to have a baby in Heaven, never be able to hold one and rock them and watch them grow up. And that's really what was bothering her. She'd given up her son because she knew she wasn't in a position to raise him herself, but now she might never see him again. And she might never have the opportunity to have another child when she was prepared.

She picked up her Bible and held it to her chest. She was so new to this, having only been a believer for less than a year, but holding the Bible had quickly become a source of comfort for her. Just the feel of the leather and the smell of the pages was usually enough to quiet her heart. With closed eyes, she whispered softly, "Lord, help me not to be angry and afraid."

Her cell phone chimed with a message as she waited for peace. She tried to ignore it and focus on listening for the still small voice, but it was no use. Her mind refused to be still tonight. Cracking one eye open, she glanced at her phone to see who had disturbed her, and then opened the other when she saw that it was Jeremy.

She'd met Jeremy on her flight to Washington from Texas, and he'd been like a guardian angel. The whole situation had been odd, especially because she generally shied away from men. Ever since the rape, she'd had an inane fear that every man was out to get her. It was often so overpowering that she would cross the street if men were coming toward her on the sidewalk or run back to her car without accomplishing whatever task she had set out to do.

Jeremy had been different. He'd sat down beside her at the airport and immediately put her at ease with his soulful eyes and kind smile. Then he'd taken care of her when they landed in Seattle, helping her navigate the crowds, reunite with her luggage, and he'd even secured her a ride to Olympia in the shuttle van. She'd felt so safe around him that she had even given him her cell number - something she never did anymore - and they had texted back and forth the last few days.

"How are you doing?" His kind words were exactly what she needed right now, but she did wonder how he knew.

She thought about how to respond. They had discussed a lot about their lives during the time in the airport, but she hadn't told him the real reason she was here or about her son. "I'm missing home." That seemed truthful and yet vague enough.

"Me too," came the reply.

Jordan smiled and felt the tension ease off her shoulders. Talking to him was just what she needed right now.

Raven tucked a strand of her midnight hair behind her ear as she regarded her reflection in the rearview mirror. She looked good - fresh - like she was wearing no makeup though in reality she was. Not a lot but enough to give her a glow. A little eyeliner, a little blush, a dab of color on her lips. Tiny pieces to make Jason notice her. Tonight was his shift at the bar, and she had every intention of going home with him when it was over.

She exited her Jeep, pulling on her miniskirt as she did to readjust it. Then she gave her top one final glance in the reflection of the mirror and smiled. She looked good. As she spun to head toward the front door, a shadow crossed her vision. What was that?

Raven peered into the darkness, suddenly wishing there were more lights in this parking lot. "Hello?" Her voice sounded scared and wimpy, not like her normal sassy self at all. She squared her shoulders and tried again, "Hello? Is anyone there?"

There was no reply, and after a moment, the breath she hadn't known she'd been holding spilled out of her lips. It was nothing. She was probably just tired. Her sleep had been restless lately. She'd always had vivid dreams, but the last few days, she'd been having some crazy nightmares, only she couldn't remember them when she woke up. All she could remember was her heart racing and fear flooding her body.

Yes, that had to be why she was seeing things. She was just tired. There was no other explanation for it. She took a deep breath, gripped her purse tighter, and entered the bar.

The dim lighting gave the place a relaxed air, but the hum of conversation made the atmosphere lively. Couples and groups filled the tables that occupied the room, but thankfully there were a few open spots at the bar which was where she wanted to be anyway.

She sidled up to the bar and leaned seductively on the edge while she waited for Jason to notice her. His eyes rounded as he turned and caught sight of her.

"Raven, what brings you here?" He looked different in his barkeep attire. The black button down shirt was so different from the t-shirt he wore at the gym, but she could still see the definition of muscles beneath the sleeves, and though seeing more of his skin at the gym was sexy, there was something about the professional attire that appealed to her even more.

Raven used her sexiest voice as she answered. "You do, actually." She bit her bottom lip and batted her eyes at him. "I thought I'd grab a drink and see if you were doing anything after your shift."

The muscles in his jaw twitched. "I'd like that, but I have an early training session at the gym tomorrow, so I've got to hit the hay as soon as I get off."

A training session on Sunday? She supposed it was possible; she'd seen his cards around the gym advertising personal sessions, and she knew he was trying to squirrel away more money. Maybe that's what she needed to do, schedule her own personal session with him. She certainly had the cash and the time.

"I understand. Do you just have one tomorrow or could you fit me in as well?" She normally didn't like spending money to get a man's attention, especially since they never lasted long, but this would not only get her some time with Jason but improve her kickboxing skills as well. Two for one.

"I can fit you in at noon if that works for you."

His lips pulled into a smile, displaying his one physical flaw - a crooked tooth. Normally perfect teeth was a must for her, but Jason had so many other positive attributes that she chose to ignore it and focus on his eyes instead. "I'll make it work. So, about that drink?"

"What's your poison?"

"Tequila. Straight." She slid onto the barstool enjoying the look of surprise that graced his features at her order. Men always underestimated her, and she enjoyed shocking them. It was too bad she wouldn't get to show Jason her other surprising talents tonight, but tomorrow wasn't that far away.

3
SUNDAY

Raven sucked in a breath and shot up in bed. Her heart hammered in her chest, and she gazed around the room trying to get her bearings. A dream. It had been a dream. Squeezing her eyes shut, she tried to hang on to whatever remnants of the dream she could, but they were fading fast. Breaking glass, screams, expressions of fear - that was all she could see.

She ran a hand across her forehead. This had to stop. She couldn't keep waking up like this every morning. Tonight, she would try sleeping pills. They had always knocked her out when she needed them, and she definitely needed them.

Her eyes shifted to the clock. Just after four a.m. Should she get up or try to get a few more hours? She wasn't meeting Jason until noon, so there was plenty of time, but she wasn't sure she could quiet her heart enough to fall back asleep.

Maybe a little television would help. Raven clicked the remote and the flat screen came to life. Of course at four in the morning, little of interest was on, but that didn't really matter. She just needed something to get her mind off the dream, so she could sleep a little longer.

Her finger paused as a smarmy looking man in a suit filled her screen. He was spouting some nonsense about Jesus filling your empty life, but it wasn't his words that had frozen her finger. No, it was the shadow she thought she saw lurking over his shoulder. Surely it was nothing - some lighting error - but it didn't look like that. The rest of the area behind him was lit up fine, so it must be her. She must be seeing things again. Raven squeezed her eyes shut and counted to ten before opening them again. When she did, the shadow was gone. Yep, pills were definitely in her future tonight.

Trepidation filled Kat as she entered the church early the next morning. What if no one here knew either? She'd spent enough hours poring over the information online to know that even among scholars, there were a lot of different views. The word rapture itself was even debated. It was all too much for her to decipher alone which was why she had texted Pastor Ron the night before and requested a sit down with him.

Pastor Ron's office was the last office down the long hallway in the administrative wing of the church. His door was open, and he sat behind the desk staring down at a book. Kat couldn't help but notice that he had no computer in the room.

Unlike most of the other pastors, Ron was older and more of a traditionalist. With his head of white hair and his full beard, he would often wear red during the month of December, and Kat had heard rumors that he took a few Santa gigs during the month every year. Kat couldn't blame him. He fit her ideal image of Santa to a tee, and his kind eyes and gentle nature only added to the perfection.

Of course, not everyone in the church found Ron as refreshing as Kat did. Because he was older, he held to more conservative values, and that turned a few of the more liberal patrons off. Enough that he was rarely asked to preach to the main congregation anymore and instead led the retired group events.

Kat didn't care about that though. What she knew was that the light of Jesus shone through this man every time he talked. Just being around him made Kat want to be a better Christian. If anyone might have the answers she sought, it would be him.

She rapped lightly on the doorframe so as not to startle him. "Pastor Ron, do you have a few minutes?"

He looked up and broke into a wide smile. "Of course, my child. Come on in. I always have time for you." He motioned to the seat across from him and Kat pulled out the chair and sat down.

The fabric was red and velvety and it reminded her of the cushion of pews, but it didn't ease her hesitation today. Her nerves still coiled tightly in her stomach. How much should she tell him? All of it? Or just enough to find out what might happen after the rapture?

Pastor Ron folded his hands together and stared at her expectantly, clearly waiting for her to speak first which made sense as she had come to him and not the other way around.

"Ahem," Kat cleared her throat. He was normally so easy to talk to, but she was afraid he might think her crazy if she said too much. She still found the situation crazy at times. "I was wondering how much you might know about the rapture."

"The rapture?" His bushy white brows lifted on his forehead. "Well, while I have studied the book of Revelation, there is nowhere in the Bible where the rapture is clearly mentioned. Most theologians believe that the verses talking about Christians meeting God in the sky are about the rapture, but no one knows for sure. Even among those who believe in the rapture, there are differing views about when it will occur."

Kat knew that all too well. Her computer was an electronic graveyard of theological debate over the rapture and the tribulation, but Micah had used the word, so she had to believe it was true. "Okay, well, let's assume it is a real thing, and for the sake of argument, let's say that believers are raptured at the beginning of the Tribulation. What happens next? What will the people left behind have to face?"

His face folded in concern. "Are you worried about your salvation, Kat?"

She shook her head. "No, not me. Not anymore, but there's a girl I am worried about. How do I convince her that all of this is real? How can I tell her what to look for if we do get raptured?"

Pastor Ron's kind brown eyes searched her soul, and for a moment, Kat thought he was going to ask her for more information. She would have given it - as crazy as it might make her sound - but she was glad when he leaned back and answered her question instead of posing his own.

"The Book of Revelation is challenging, but there are a few things we do know. It is clear there will be wars and famine and much more death than we are used to seeing. A leader will emerge who will claim to unite the world in peace. He will be the anti-Christ, but many will follow his false teachings as he will probably be very charismatic and charming. At some point, he will require people to take his mark. There is much debate on whether this is an actual mark or just the act of worshipping him. I tend to believe it will be literal but some disagree. And there will be two witnesses who will be killed and then rise again."

Kat blinked as she took it all in. "Okay, wars, famine, death, a leader, and witnesses. That's all I can give her?" It all sounded so vague. How was she going to convince Raven of the coming tribulation when the signs were so ambiguous one could claim they were happening even now. Minus the witnesses, of course.

"There are other things mentioned, but it is unclear whether they are literal or metaphorical. I don't want you to pass along something as truth that might be a metaphor." He leaned forward and caught her eyes again. "You tell your friend to watch for these things. I know they seem vague, but these wars will be unlike any we have seen before. They will be hard to ignore when they begin happening, and anyone who listened and read will understand what they mean."

"Thank you, Pastor Ron. I'll pass this on to her." A long sigh slipped past Kat's lips. "Hopefully, she won't be so hard-headed that she doesn't listen." She pushed back her chair to stand, but Pastor Ron stopped her with a hand on her arm.

"Before you go, can I pray for you?"

Kat nodded though the experience of people praying for her still felt odd and unnatural. Still, with what she'd been tasked with, she figured she could use all the help she could get.

Jordan wandered into the kitchen, expecting to find Kat staring at her laptop again, but the room was empty. "Hello?" she called out in case Kat was in another room, but no return answer came. Where was she?

Jordan crossed to the cabinet to grab a bowl for some cereal and then turned to the fridge for the milk. A note attached to the door gave her pause. It was written in Kat's familiar scrawl.

"Went to church early to ask Pastor Ron some questions, but I'll swing back by to pick you up by ten."

Well, that explained her absence then. Jordan hoped Pastor Ron would have some answers for them. While she was glad to be doing God's work, doing it blind was stressful. Some sort of roadmap or outline would certainly help.

After pouring the milk into her bowl, she crossed to the small dinette table and sat down. Kat's kitchen was homey, decorated in a soft mauve color with gold accents, but it still felt empty without her there. Kat had invited her to stay and told her to make herself at home, but that didn't make Jordan feel any less like she was infringing on Kat's space.

Jordan bowed her head and closed her eyes to pray, but before she could utter a word, a vision flooded her mind. A baby, wrapped in a blue cloth, lay crying in a crib. A blue bear lay next to him, but no one appeared to be coming to his rescue. Who was this baby and why was he crying? Suddenly, the vision shifted, and she saw a dark shape leaning over the crib. Though she could see no face, the fear emanating from the baby thundered through her body, sending her heart rate through the roof. Her throat constricted, making it hard to breathe, and then as suddenly as it appeared, the vision was gone.

Jordan shivered as she tried to make sense of the vision. It was so unlike anything else she had ever seen. There were no words to say, no sins to share, but she felt in her bones that the baby - whoever and wherever he was - was in trouble.

"Who is he, God? What do I need to do?" But there was no response. She would just have to wait. Perhaps this vision was going to come in bits and pieces like the vision that had led her to Kat had. Hopefully there would be more because she wasn't sure she would rest until she knew that the baby was okay.

❧ 4 ❧

MONDAY

"I just don't understand, Dr. Jameson, how could I have breast cancer? I'm so young."

Kat smiled sympathetically at Lindsey, the young woman across from her. Twenty-six was awfully young to have breast cancer, but Kat had checked the results twice just to be sure. "It is rare in someone your age, but there are some things that could have raised your risks. Do you mind if I ask you some questions?"

Lindsey shrugged, but her eyes still swam with questions. "Can't hurt I suppose. Will it help you know how to treat me?"

"It might." Kat chose her words carefully. As an oncologist, she had learned long ago not to give too much hope until she knew how the cancer was responding. She looked down at the list of risks on her iPad; she could cross off obesity and age. Lindsey was not overweight nor was she over the age of fifty. "Do you remember what age you were when you first got your period?"

Lindsey's eyes squeezed shut sending tiny crow's feet lines out from the corners. It would be years before the lines resided there permanently, but Kat could see where they would lay. "Um, thirteen, I think. Before high school for sure."

So, after twelve probably. She moved to the next risk. "Have you ever been on birth control pills?" Kat knew from the medical intake form that Lindsey wasn't on them currently, but she was a new patient to Kat.

"Yeah, in high school and the first few years of college. Probably six years total. Until I switched to the shot. Do the pills increase the risk of breast cancer?"

Kat nodded as she marked that risk factor. "Some of them can. Do you remember which ones you were on?"

Lindsey shook her head. "No, that was four years ago. Can you find out from my old doctor though?"

"Of course. How about drinking? Do you drink alcohol on a regular basis?" Lindsey was still in college pursuing a masters, so Kat had no doubt she drank. The question was how much.

"Define regular." Lindsey bit her lip and shifted in the chair. The question obviously hit a little close to home.

"Do you have a drink every day?"

Lindsey's eyes slid to the side. "Not every day."

"Okay, and when you drink, how many do you have?"

"Are you saying alcohol increases the risk too?" A note of anger laced Lindsey's voice as if she didn't believe what Kat was suggesting.

"It does, depending on how much and how often you drink. So, how many do you have when you drink?" Kat took a deep breath and forced herself to remain calm. She'd been in college once - never been a big drinker but she'd seen plenty of girls who were. Even though it was regrettable, she knew it was a large part of college life, especially for those involved in sororities or fraternities.

Lindsey's eyes dropped to her arm and followed her right hand as it scratched absently at her left arm. "I don't know. Two or three maybe. More if it's a party, but those are only on weekends."

Two or three a day? The admission saddened Kat, but she could believe it from the number of patients she saw who had anxiety disorders. What did these kids have to be so anxious about? Well, a lot actually, but she doubted most of them knew that angels and demons were all around them and preparing for a war.

Kat marked the risk box and sighed as she read the next one. Somehow she just knew Lindsey's answer would be yes, and if she was bothered by the alcohol question, this certainly wouldn't go over any better. "Have you terminated any pregnancies?"

Lindsey's head snapped up. "Terminated? You mean

like abortions? Are you allowed to ask me that? Do I have to answer?"

"No," Kat said with a sigh as she tapped the risk factor. "You don't have to answer the question, but I am trying to help you here, Lindsey. Though there are conflicting opinions, there have been studies that show a link between breast cancer and abortions. I'm not saying that's the cause here, but it is a standard medical question. You can choose not to answer it, but being open about your medical history allows me to diagnose and treat you properly."

Fire burned out of Lindsey's eyes as she grabbed her purse from the floor and stood. "What are you? Some kind of religious nut? You're supposed to be curing my cancer, not pushing your morality on me."

"I wasn't-" But Kat knew it was too late. Lindsey was already at the door of her office, and with an exaggerated yank, she flung the door open and marched into the hall. Great. No doubt she would be hearing from her supervisor later about this.

Kat rubbed a hand across her forehead. Perhaps she should have just skipped the question. She certainly didn't need to be building walls between herself and others. Lindsey hadn't had the glow around her, but did that mean she was already saved? Or that she couldn't be saved? Kat refused to believe people couldn't be saved, but she had no idea why some people had the glow and others didn't. Once again, she wished she had been thinking clearly when Micah told her about all of this. There was so much she didn't know, and she feared she was making things worse stumbling around in the dark.

With a sigh, Kat dropped her head to her hands. Perhaps a moment of prayer would give her some clarity and the strength to follow up on the next patient.

Jordan squared her shoulders and inhaled deeply as she pulled open the front door of the pregnancy center. This would be her first day on the job here, and while she was excited, she was also a little nervous. She'd worked at a pregnancy center back in Texas, from the day she decided to put her son up for adoption, and she enjoyed the work. But back there, she'd had visions of the women she would see that day before they even entered her office, but there'd been no vision today. In fact, she'd had no vision since the one of the baby yesterday, so she had no idea what to expect.

The reception area of the center was warm and inviting. Neutral colors accented with blue and pink pillows on the comfy couches created a homey atmosphere. Even the receptionist's desk added to the ambiance instead of detracting from it.

"Can I help you?" the woman behind the desk asked. She was young looking, though older than Jordan. Late twenties maybe. Her blonde hair was pulled up in a loose bun, and a pen was wedged between her ear and head.

"Hi, I'm Jordan Wright. I'm a transfer from Texas. It's my first day."

A smile lit up the woman's face. "Jordan, hi. I'm Lana. Let me ring Carla, the boss, for you, and she'll get you set up."

Jordan nodded and took a seat next to a woman with a growing belly on the beige couch, but it wasn't long before a dark-skinned woman with beautiful curls opened the door and called her back.

"Jordan, I'm Carla." She extended a slender hand which Jordan shook. "Grace told me all about you. Let me show you to your office."

"Thank you, and thank you for allowing me to work here on such short notice. I really enjoyed working for Grace and appreciated that she was willing to vouch for me." Grace had been her boss back in Texas and when Jordan had told her she had to go to Washington state for an undetermined amount of time, Grace had reached out to Carla and secured her this job.

The smile that Carla flashed could have lit up a dark room. "We are always in need of help here. There are so many women who need us, but we are so few." She opened the door to a small and very bare office. It held only a desk, computer, phone, and guest chairs. "I'm sorry it's not more, but you can make it your own."

Jordan shook her head. "This is perfect. I don't need bells and whistles, just a comfortable place to share my heart."

"I'll let you get situated then and bring in the papers I need you to sign. Our program is the same one you used in Texas and I've left log on credentials in the top drawer. Go ahead and get logged in. You can start seeing clients after lunch."

Jordan thanked Carla and crossed to the desk. Her office back in Texas had pictures of all the women she had helped and their babies. She wished she had remembered to bring some with her so this place didn't feel so sterile, but she would start fresh. Surely, she would acquire some to begin a wall here as well.

Raven pulled into the gym parking lot and turned off her Jeep. She hoped she would get some time with Jason before class. Her plan had been to turn her charm on him yesterday during the personal training session, but he seemed determined to push her and not chat. Probably, that had something to do with his first client staying late and the client after her coming in early. They'd only had a few minutes alone, but Raven was determined to find some time with him today.

She checked her appearance in the mirror. The workout

would undo the masterpiece she had worked so hard on, but that was fine. She'd have a few minutes to turn his head. As long as the new girl wasn't around.

Kat. The name felt dirty in her mouth, and she rolled her eyes. The girl had come in a week ago with her fresh face and sparkly smile, and she'd turned Jason's eye. He'd spent more time critiquing her on the bags lately than he ever had speaking with Raven, and it had to stop.

She glanced one more time in the mirror before flipping up the visor, but her hand paused. What the heck was that? Raven whipped around but there was nothing there. She could have sworn she had seen a black shape move past her window, but nothing was in the car.

Nerves. It was probably nerves. With Kat in the picture, Raven would have to try harder to entice Jason, and she wasn't used to having to try so hard. She knew she was pretty. With her thin figure, long dark hair, and ice blue eyes, she attracted men's attention - had since she was twelve when her stepfather's eyes wandered to her more than they should have. That had been the worst year of her life, but she'd learned something. She'd learned how to use her assets to get what she wanted from men. And now she wanted Jason, but he was proving harder to charm.

There was nothing extremely special about Jason except that he was different from her normal tastes. He wasn't wealthy, but his physical prowess was impressive. Mostly though, she figured it was the challenge he was presenting. Raven generally just had to bat her eyes and drop a few suggestive hints to get what she wanted, but that had become boring and predictable. So, when Jason didn't seem affected by her usual antics, the challenge of winning him had become exciting. She didn't know if it was because he worked at the gym and didn't like to mix business with pleasure or if there was another reason, but once she set her mind on something, she didn't let it go. And she wasn't going to let him go either.

As she opened the car door and stepped out, a weird feeling of unease like cold fingertips on bare flesh trickled up her arms. Raven shivered and glanced around, but no one else was even in the parking lot. She had arrived early in hopes of seeing Jason, and only three other cars were even in the lot.

There was a blue truck, a green Mustang, and a gold Honda. All were empty, but Raven couldn't shake the feeling that someone else or something else was out here with her. She scoured the lot one more time, but saw nothing. No person, no animal, and certainly no black shape. She was losing it.

Her sleep was to blame. She just knew it. Even with the sleeping pills last night, her sleep had been restless, and she'd woken up exhausted and scared just like the last few mornings. Her dreams appeared to be getting even more vivid though she still couldn't recall them. Tiny pieces would flicker briefly in her mind before blowing out like a candle, and all she could ever remember was that she'd been scared. Scared and confused. Much like now. But they were just feelings. They meant nothing.

With a final glance around the parking lot, Raven shouldered her bag, locked her car, and headed into the gym.

Brian, the owner, sat behind the desk, his cell phone plastered to his ear. Lately, it seemed like that's all he did - talk on the phone. Supposedly, he was working on getting the next fight card ready, but all Raven knew was that she was paying for instruction and often didn't get it because he had to run off to answer a call. As far as she was concerned, Brian either needed to hire more instructors or someone to organize his fight card so he could instruct.

He nodded as she passed, and she flashed him a small wave. Brian wasn't her concern right now. Her eyes scoured the room for Jason, but he wasn't in the main room. The weight room then? That would actually be better. It was smaller there and she could use the excuse of asking him to show her how to lift properly to engage him.

She stuck her head into the weight room and smiled as she saw Jason stacking weights on the bench press. Perfect. She would change quickly and then return to work her magic.

Five minutes later, she was changed and heading back toward the weight room. "Hey you," she said to Jason as she entered. "I was looking for you." The room was small

and packed full of equipment. Because the gym had originally been a garage and a butcher shop before that, it
wasn't really built for a weight room. That didn't keep
Brian, however, from picking up every piece of used
equipment he could find and shoving it in the room. Raven
knew he used some of it, but dust littered some of the older
pieces and she wondered why Brian kept them in the room.

Jason looked up from the chest press bench, and she bit
her lip to keep from smiling as his eyes took in her tight
leggings and tank. She could tell he appreciated the view.
"Hey, Raven. What can I do for you?"

"Well, I really want to work on my chest muscles, but I
haven't lifted in a long time. I was hoping you could tell
me what might be the best place to start." Raven pushed
her lower lip out in the faintest pout and batted her eyes
at him.

"Uh, sure. The bench press is pretty good for that, and
I just finished. Let me take the weights off and we'll see
how you do with the bar." He turned his back to her as he
began removing the large circular weights from the bar.

"I'm sure I can handle some weight." Raven was
aiming for a light, teasing tone, but it bothered her that
Jason thought she was too weak to lift a bar with weights.
"I'm not a total newbie." Men often underestimated her,
but she hadn't thought he'd been like that. Especially after
she'd survived his one-on-one training yesterday.

He pulled a thirty-five pound weight off the bar and

leaned it against the wall before turning to her. "I didn't say you were, but if you haven't lifted in a while, the best place to start is with the bar. Then we can see how easy it is and adjust from there."

Raven wanted to argue, but she knew that wouldn't earn her any bonus points with him, and the point was to win him over - not win the argument, besides she was enjoying watching his muscles as he moved the weights. She tugged on a strand of hair and pouted her lips slightly. "Okay, you're the trainer. I'm sure you know best."

He raised an eyebrow at her as if he wasn't sure if she were telling the truth or attempting to stroke his ego by telling him what he wanted to hear. "Yeah, I am." After pulling the weight off the other side, he patted the bench. "Okay, come lie down here."

Raven smiled as she lay back on the bench. "Like this?" she asked, placing her hands on the bar.

"Yes, like that. Now push the bar up and let's see if you can do a complete rep." He kept his hands under the bar as she pushed it up and lowered it to her chest before placing it back in the holders.

"See. I told you I'm not a newbie."

A slight smile pulled at his lips, and he rolled his eyes. "Okay, you're right. Let me add ten pounds on." He moved toward the weight rack with careful steps and grabbed two five pound weights. Then he added one to each side. "Let's try this."

Raven was surprised at how much pressure ten pounds added, but she tried not to show it on her face as she lowered the bar and then pressed it up again.

"So, this new girl, Kat. What do you think of her?" Jason asked.

Anger surged through Raven, and she forced herself to focus on the rep so she didn't drop the bar and crush herself. Was he really asking her about some other girl? She gritted her teeth and forced her voice to stay even and not betray the venom she was brewing inside. "I don't know; she seems odd."

He nodded, but his eyes weren't on her. They were focused on something Raven couldn't see - something not even in the room. Was he picturing Kat's face? "Yeah, odd. I can see that. She told me my life had purpose last week. It was so weird because I'd been thinking about how it didn't. How this was all I had-" he gestured around the small room. "No wife, no dog, no real savings. Just the gym and my bartending gig on weekends."

"You don't think that's enough?" Raven didn't think it was enough, especially not for someone in his thirties, but she wasn't planning to settle down with Jason; she just wanted to have a little fun and let off some steam. In fact, Raven doubted she would ever settle down - letting a man be in charge of her was not something she ever wanted to do - but that didn't mean she couldn't find some enjoyment along the way.

He looked down at her. "No. I don't. I'm almost thirty-five, Raven, and while I love my job, this was not how I saw myself growing up. I know I probably look like I have it together, but I'm a mess. I drink - every night, and I sleep until noon or later. It was like Kat saw all of that and knew just what to say to me even though she barely knows me."

"Yeah, that is weird." Raven pursed her lips together. If Kat could read people that well, winning Jason's attention back might be harder than she thought. "You think she's clairvoyant or something?"

"I don't know," he said. "Maybe she's just really good at reading people, but it was definitely strange. Nice, but strange."

Raven didn't like the tone his voice had taken or the faraway gleam in his eyes. She needed to figure out who this Kat girl was and stop her before she captivated Jason completely.

5
TUESDAY

"Good morning, Dr. Jameson," Stephanie, the receptionist for the floor, said as Kat neared. Stephanie had been one of the first people Kat had seen lights around, but though she had said the words that came into her head - words of affirmation on her job - the light hadn't left Stephanie. Kat wondered what else she needed to say.

"Good morning, Stephanie." Kat looked both directions before leaning closer and lowering her voice. "Is there anything I can do for you? Anything I can pray for?"

Stephanie's eyes widened, and she shook her head. "I don't think you want to go around asking questions like that."

"Why not?"

Stephanie's face twitched, and she swallowed audibly

before pulling a small piece of paper from her stack. "Because Dr. Damon wants to see you, and he didn't sound happy."

Kat sighed. She'd known this was coming. Even though she'd said nothing religious to Lindsey, she'd known from the girl's reaction that her probing questions were going to get her in trouble, but they were part of the standard medical history and not asking them wouldn't give her the whole picture which could affect treatment.

"Thanks, Stephanie. I'll go see him, but I meant what I said. If you need anything, please let me know. You can always call my cell if you don't feel comfortable talking here."

"Thank you, Dr. Jameson. I might take you up on that."

Kat had no doubt she would. If she still had a light around her, she could only assume it was because she hadn't made the decision to follow Jesus completely yet. Of course, she had no idea what happened when people did make the decision. Did the light disappear? How she wished Micah had given her a few more instructions before disappearing.

She dropped her purse in her office and then continued down the hall to Dr. Damon's office. He was the head of the oncology department and though he rarely saw patients anymore, he oversaw all of her cases and those of the other doctors on the floor. She presumed he then had to report to the hospital board, but she'd never been curious enough to ask.

She knocked on Dr. Damon's door, pushing it open when he answered from within. Memories of entering the principal's office in a similar way when in school flooded her mind, and she pushed them away. He wasn't going to give her detention - a verbal reprimand maybe or a write up in her file but nothing more.

"Ah, Dr. Jameson. I see you got my message."

His voice grated on her nerves. It held that nasally tone of someone who thought they were superior to everyone else. "I did. What can I do for you, sir?"

He motioned to the chair across from him. "Please sit. It appears we need to discuss the handling of one of your cases."

Kat sat gingerly in the chair though her flight instinct made her want to keep standing. "Let me guess, Lindsey Gates?"

His left eyebrow cocked as he placed his hands together like he was about to pray. It was too bad she knew that wasn't his next step. "I see you are aware of your misstep then?"

Kat bit the inside of her cheek and took a deep breath before answering. "It wasn't a misstep. It was a standard medical question. I am trying to determine the best treat-ment for her and the way to do that is to get all the pertinent medical information. I informed her that she didn't have to answer the question."

His face folded into a snide expression of insincerity, and his fingertips tapped against each other. "Now, Dr. Jameson, Ms. Gates claims that you insinuated a termination could be a risk factor for her early cancer. As you are well aware, the medical community does not believe that terminations are a risk factor for cancer."

Kat's fingers dug into her thigh to keep from shaking. "The medical community also once denied the risk between smoking and cancer if you remember. Back in the thirties and forties, cigarette companies used to use doctor promotions in their ads because no link had been discovered yet. There are in fact several published studies that have declared a link between abortions and cancer that would disagree with you."

"Ridiculous fanatical religious studies. Surely, you don't believe they hold any worth." He'd phrased it as a question, but it was clear that he expected her answer to be no.

"I understand that the topic is still heated and that family history is still the biggest cause, but according to her intake form, no one in her family has been diagnosed with cancer. Now, she isn't overweight, but she has been on the pill and she does drink. Those are also both risk factors, so my asking about her terminations wasn't to place blame; it was to determine a clear medical history so that I can come up with the best treatment plan for her."

"But you do believe terminations could be a risk factor?"

Kat let her breath out slowly to keep herself calm. "The studies have shown that hormone disruption may be a link. Now that can come from being on the pill, waiting longer to have kids, not breastfeeding, or terminating a pregnancy. I'm simply unwilling to rule it out as a possibility until we know more."

He sighed. "I was hoping that you would come to see the error of your ways, but as you are clearly deluded, you are now a liability for the department. I have no choice but to place you on administrative leave until the board comes to a decision."

Kat's jaw dropped. "What? You can't put me on leave simply because you don't like a question I asked."

His snide smile returned. "Actually, Dr. Jameson, I can. This, along with your religious discussions that have been documented as occurring during company time and the instances of you being seen speaking to someone no one else could see in the last few weeks, allows me to make this decision. Whether it is temporary or final remains up to the board, but I will be taking over your current cases for now. You're dismissed."

Kat wanted to argue, to plead her case, but then Micah's words sounded in her brain. "This world is not your kingdom. Your kingdom is in Heaven, and your job is to tell people about Jesus." She supposed she'd known even then that she might lose her job, but she hadn't expected it to happen so quickly.

"Understood. I'll gather my things and be out of your hair shortly." Though she could feel the tears building in her eyes, she refused to cry in front of him. With all the dignity she could muster, she rose from the chair and walked out of his office with her head held high.

Jordan took a deep breath before answering the woman who sat across from her. This wasn't going to be easy.

"Samantha, I know you are worried about your husband finding out about your affair-"

The woman's gasp interrupted Jordan, and her hand flew to her mouth. Fear radiated from her wide eyes. Jordan waited for the question she knew would come.

"How did you know about my affair?" Samantha's constricted voice was not much louder than a whisper. Gone was the brazen young woman who had entered with abortion on her mind.

Jordan wondered what had made her come to the Options Pregnancy Clinic in the first place. Hadn't Samantha realized they didn't promote abortion here? "I could tell you, but I don't think you'd believe me."

"Did my husband hire you? Does he have some sort of camera watching us now?"

Jordan shook her head. "Samantha, I don't know your husband. This is actually only my second day on the job here. Look, this is going to be hard to believe, but I know about your affair because I have visions."

Samantha leaned back in the chair and Jordan recognized the apprehensive look that covered her face. She'd seen it often. Right now, Samantha thought she was crazy, but it was about to get much worse.

"About a year ago, I was raped. I considered abortion too until I had a vision of my unborn child - my son. Then I knew I couldn't kill him, but I couldn't raise him either, so I gave him up for adoption. Afterwards, I felt empty, and I asked God to help me, to use me. The next day I began having visions of other people. People I needed to talk to. I had one of you this morning."

Samantha shook her head slowly, but Jordan continued. She knew she was close to the woman believing now. "I could give you his name and details of your meetings, but I'd rather not. What I can tell you is this - if you abort this baby, you will be haunted by guilt and your marriage will fall apart anyway."

"But I can't tell him."

"You can. Your husband will be sad and angry, but he's a good God-fearing man, and he will forgive you, but then you have to decide to choose the right path. You have to let the other man go."

Samantha stared at her a moment longer before swallowing hard and nodding. The look of apprehension still lay on her face, but Jordan could see in her eyes that she believed.

"Thank you, I think," Samantha said as she gathered her purse and stood.

"I know it isn't easy, and I'll be here for you whenever you need, but it's the right thing, Samantha."

Samantha nodded one more time and then exited Jordan's office. Jordan sighed. This never got easier. Suddenly, searing pain filled her head, and she squeezed her eyes shut. Her hands flew to her temple as if they could keep it from pounding.

The baby came into focus again. He was still crying, and the black shape was there. Only this time it was more solid - a person or at least a person-like shape. Claw-like hands reached into the crib and picked the baby up, and his cries intensified. Jordan screamed as the face of the shape came into focus, and then her world went dark.

Raven narrowed her eyes at Kat who was punching a bag across the room. She looked so innocent, so pure, but Raven knew there had to be more going on behind the pretty face. There had to be dark secrets lurking in her closet - things she wouldn't want anyone to know. She'd learned the hard way that everyone had secrets, no matter how hard they tried to pretend otherwise, and the ones who tried the hardest usually had the darkest secrets.

"Earth to Raven. You going to workout today?"

Raven turned her attention back to Lilly, her mitt partner for the day. Lilly was a nice kid, fourteen and goofy. Her long blonde hair was pulled back in a ponytail and swung a lazy pendulum behind her back with every movement.

Raven remembered fourteen, but she hadn't been goofy and fresh faced. By fourteen, she'd already been passed around to her father's friends at least once. She'd experienced pregnancy and an abortion along with all the guilt and fear and hatred that accompanied it. A part of her envied Lilly - her childhood, her innocence. She might have struggles in her life, but Raven doubted it was anything like her own.

"Yeah, sorry." She glanced toward the board to read the combination Brian had written.

"What's your deal with Kat anyway? She seems nice. A little obsessed with Jon maybe, but nice."

"What do you mean?" Raven threw the jab-cross-hook combination before letting her eyes slide to Kat once again. Her focus didn't seem to be on Jon at the moment who was busting out some random combination with his best friend on the other side of the gym.

"Probably nothing. She was just talking the other day about his light."

"His light?" Was this Kat girl crazy? That might be just the chink Raven was looking for. People didn't like crazy. It scared them. Jab-jab-hook and a roll.

Lilly shrugged and moved to match Raven's new position. "I don't know what she meant by that. Probably just that he was so good, but she watched him for like five minutes. I told her he was going to think she had the hots for him."

Raven doubted that. She didn't know Jon well, but he was one of the most focused boxers she'd ever seen. He rarely even spoke to people at the gym - except for his friend, Jesse. The two of them would come in, do their own routine or Brian's occasionally, and then leave. Kat could probably stare at him the whole class and he wouldn't notice.

"What did she say to that?" Raven asked as she threw the final combination of the round.

"Nothing, but she stopped staring at him."

Was it possible Raven had it wrong? That Kat didn't have an eye for Jason? The girl had denied it, but Raven trusted people about as far as she could throw them. It didn't matter. Kat was a thorn in her side no matter who she liked and Raven was determined to get rid of her.

Kat stood as the teapot whistled. She was glad for the excuse to do something else. She'd spent too long sitting and thinking about her suspension. What in the world was she supposed to do with all this free time? She hadn't had so much time on her hands since before she'd first gone to college. If Stella were still alive, perhaps they could spend the time shopping or dining at restaurants they had never had a chance to eat at before. But Stella wasn't still alive, and her death had triggered all of this - the lights, Kat talking to an angel, her sharing her beliefs. It was so crazy how her life had changed in less than a month.

"Is that tea?"

Kat jumped at the sound of Jordan's voice and was glad she hadn't already had the kettle in hand. Spilling hot water on herself sounded as appealing as... well, as being suspended actually.

"It will be," Kat said as Jordan fell into a chair at the table. Something was off about her. Her face was pale, and her shoulders curled forward as if pressed by an invisible weight. Had she had as bad a day as Kat had?

"Shall I pour you some?" But Kat already knew what Jordan's answer would be. Before she'd started her job, Jordan would wake every morning at six and spend an hour reading and praying. Kat didn't usually have to get up that early, but the sounds of someone else in her house had woken her the first morning, so she'd decided to join Jordan.

The girl's breakfast consisted of cereal, a banana, and a cup of tea. Lunch would be a sandwich or a salad, complemented with another cup of tea. Kat had no doubt that's what she had packed yesterday and today for lunch as well even though she had eaten it at her work.

Though not English, around four o'clock, she would fill another cup of tea and sip it as she read or worked a crossword puzzle. At six, she would begin making dinner or ask Kat how she could help if Kat had already started. The dishes would be washed and put away shortly after dinner and then Jordan would either read or watch a little TV. Kat had often wondered how Jordan had taken time out of her routine to find Kat if she was this methodical, but perhaps it was more a reaction to living in an unknown place than how she was normally.

"Please. It was an exceptionally hard day today."

Kat glanced over her shoulder to see Jordan rubbing her temples. The girl didn't often show her fatigue, but Kat knew her visions had been getting worse or stranger. Jordan hadn't seemed her usual cheerful self since church on Sunday, but Kat had no idea why. She'd assumed it was the nervousness of starting a new job, but now she wasn't so sure. At times like these, she wished she had Jordan's gift, so she could have a little insight. Neither of the girls' gift was all that pleasant, and on most days, Kat figured she would take her lights over Jordan's visions any day, but right now she wished she could see what was bothering the girl.

"What happened today?"

Jordan sighed as she pulled her knees to her chest and wrapped her arms around them. "Met a woman today who wanted to have an abortion so that her husband wouldn't know about her affair."

"Whoa, that is heavy." Kat poured the water into two mugs and then carried them to the table.

Jordan picked up her mug, blew softly into it, and then took a sip and shook her head. "I know I get these visions to help people, but sometimes I wish I didn't have to know all the dirt."

"Did she change her mind and decide to keep the baby?"

"I think so. She said she would think about it." Jordan blew out a heavy breath. "I love helping these women, but seeing them reminds me so much of my son."

Jordan had mentioned her son briefly, but more as an explanation for her visions than details about him. Kat had questions about him, about the experience, but Jordan hadn't seemed open to sharing more at the time. Kat figured she would open up when she felt comfortable, but she did wonder if Jordan had gotten to hold him before she gave him up. "Do you ...miss him?"

A sad smile spread across Jordan's lips. "Every day.

Especially now with the rapture hanging over us. I just wish I could see him one more time, you know?"

Kat understood that feeling. Though she had no children of her own and knew that bond was different than what she felt for her best friend, she would give anything to see Stella again. "I hear that, but you know you will in Heaven, right?" Ugh, why was she using those words with Jordan? They hadn't helped her when she had been hurting, so why did she think they would help Jordan?

Jordan bit her lip and turned the mug in a slow circle. "There's more though. Sunday, before you picked me up, I had a vision of a baby. He was crying and a dark shape stood over his crib, but that was all I got."

Kat's brow furrowed. She'd never received visions - only dreams - and she was certainly no expert on Jordan's visions, but from what the girl had told her, that did seem odd. "Does that normally happen?"

Jordan shook her head. "No, normally, I get the whole scenario. Who I'm supposed to talk to, what I'm supposed to tell them, what secret information I'll need to let them know I'm telling the truth. The only other time I've received partial visions was when I was coming to find you. I got them in spurts like I first saw you yelling out the window and crying while it rained. That wasn't enough information, so I asked for more, and I got the feeling that I was supposed to come see you, but all I received was Washington state. Then on the plane, I received Olympia, and then in the hotel, I got a vision of Patrick. I guess they came that way, so I couldn't ask questions and would just follow the prompting."

She sighed before continuing, "Sunday, all I got was the baby and the dark shape, but then I didn't get a vision Monday morning like I normally do. I had another vision of the baby today. Only this time, the dark shape had form, and I saw claw-like hands lift the baby up." Her eyes fixed Kat with an intense stare. "I think that baby may be my son, Kat, and I think he's in trouble."

"Okay, let's pray about it and see if God shows us what we need to do."

"But why would he be in trouble, Kat? I thought we were supposed to be saving people old enough to make their own decision about God. My son isn't even a year old. He can't even talk."

Kat placed her hand on Jordan's arm. "Look, this is all new. The world as we knew it is changing, so all we can do is trust and pray, right?"

Jordan sniffed and wiped a tear from the corner of her eye. "You're right. I'm just so scared."

I am too, Kat thought to herself, but she didn't say it aloud. She needed to be Jordan's rock right now. Her own fears could wait, couldn't they?

❦ 6 ❦

WEDNESDAY

ordan stared at the woman across from her and waited for the vision to come. It never took this long, but then again, her visions had been different the last few days. And this morning, for the first time in months, she'd received nothing. She'd forgotten what silence was after months of visions every morning, and she'd stayed on her knees an extra twenty minutes which was ridiculous because it wasn't like God was late. So, what was going on?

Actually, it had been silent since the vision of the baby yesterday which only deepened her concern that the baby was her son. If these visions were like the ones that drove her to find Kat, they would not go away until she went to find her son, but what if she was wrong? She had just started this new job, and Micah had told Kat they had work to do here. What if she was just hoping the baby was her son so she had an excuse to go see him?

"Excuse me. Aren't you supposed to show me pamphlets or something."

Jordan blinked and returned her focus to the girl across from her. She was young, probably under seventeen. Maybe she'd received nothing because the girl had nothing to hide? But that made no sense because she was pregnant, and Jordan doubted she would be here if she weren't afraid of what her parents would say when they found out.

"Right." Jordan grabbed the stack that sat next to her computer. "Do you know how far along you are?"

The girl shook her head, and from the twist of her mouth, Jordan was fairly certain she was biting the inside of her lip as she did. "Not that far. I'm three weeks late, and I took the test a few days ago." The girl's hands lay in her lap, but they were not still - clasping and unclasping with nervous energy.

"Okay, well we offer testing and ultrasounds here. We'd start with a urine test to be positive. Ultrasounds are usually scheduled about week ten or twelve. It's hard to see much before then."

The girl's mouth fell open. "You can see the baby at twelve weeks?"

Jordan smiled, but it always surprised her how little these women seemed to understand about fetal development. Had they never learned this in school? "To be fair, the baby looks a lot like a kidney bean on the ultrasound, but it's definitely a baby with fingers, toes, and a heartbeat."

All color faded from the girl's face and her hand snaked up to tug on her collar as if it had suddenly become too tight. "I don't think I can raise a baby. I'm only sixteen."

"I completely understand, but that's why there's adoption. There are so many people out there who are unable to have children of their own, and they would love to adopt your baby. In some cases, they even pay for all the medical care."

"Adoption? You mean give the baby up? How could I do that?"

It never ceased to amaze Jordan how women could rationalize that it was better to kill their baby than give them life and let someone love on him or her. "It's hard, but it's so much better than the alternative."

The girl stopped tugging on her collar and focused on Jordan. "You gave your baby up for adoption?"

"I did. Back in Texas. I was like you - young and unable to care for a baby, so I found an amazing couple and gave him to them. You could do the same."

"But don't you miss him?" The girl's voice was quiet, pinched.

"Every day," Jordan said, "but at least I know he's alive and he has a chance to have a wonderful life."

Except he didn't. Jordan knew that now. With the rapture imminent, he would never get to grow up. Was that what was bothering her? Was that why her visions were focused on this baby? Because she was too obsessed with her own son and how little of life he would get to live? She supposed it was possible, but racing off to Texas to make sure he was okay seemed silly. Still, something was definitely going on with her. The question was what was she supposed to do about it?

Kat hoisted her bag higher on her shoulder as she pulled open the glass door to the gym. A month ago, she would never have believed she would have enjoyed spending an hour in a giant padded room punching a bag and sweating like a linebacker, but there was something freeing in the workout. The ability to let out all of her frustrations was satisfying, and even though she was now dealing with Stella's death better, she had even more frustrations with this new task and her suspension.

She was going stir-crazy sitting at home, but it was easier than what she knew she should be doing - getting out and sharing her faith with people. She'd always found it hard to share about her faith, especially with those she didn't know, but now the stakes felt much higher and the pressure was heavy. This hour allowed her to escape it for a short moment in time, at least when she wasn't seeing lights over the people in the gym.

"Hey, how are you enjoying the gym?" The gravelly voice pulled her from her thoughts and she looked up to see Brian, the owner of the gym, staring at her from behind his desk. His sleeveless t-shirt showed off his muscular arms, and though she couldn't currently see his legs, she knew he would be sporting a pair of tights under shorts. But it wasn't his outfit that caught her attention, it was the light behind him.

Great. She needed to talk to him now? Though she couldn't be certain, Kat didn't think he'd had a light any other time she'd been in the gym. Was Micah trying to take everything away from her? She couldn't lose the gym as well as her job. It was her place of sanity. She'd gone crazy this morning just sitting around the house after Jordan left for work. "It's good. I'm really enjoying it."

"Good. It's Kate, right?"

She smiled slightly. That was a mistake she received often, but she couldn't fault him. Other than the few minutes they had chatted when she signed her contract, this was the longest conversation she'd had with him. He was usually working with the more advanced people - like Raven. "It's Kat, actually."

"Kat, right. Sorry. Well, I'm glad you're here." He smiled at her, but something in his expression told her he wasn't quite done with the conversation yet.

"Uh, thanks." She considered him a moment as she thought of how best to approach the subject. He was someone she was supposed to talk to, but she knew so little about him. How was she supposed to start a conversation about his faith when she didn't even know if he had a family?

"Can I ask you a question?" He seemed as surprised by his question as she was, but Kat recovered first, smiling and nodding. This had to be her cue.

She placed her bag on the floor and sat on one of the chairs across from his desk. "What can I do for you?"

He took a deep breath, then his eyes shifted to the desk and then out the window. Traffic flowed steadily by on the busy street out the window, and a few pedestrians strolled the sidewalk, but Kat knew the view wasn't why his gaze was focused that direction. He was gathering the courage to speak, so Kat waited patiently. "I've heard a little about the conversations you've had with some of the members here."

Uh oh, was he about to tell her she couldn't talk to people about their faith? He didn't seem like the type to lay down conditions like that, but she knew that a lot of the people in this gym didn't believe like she did, and even those who claimed to, didn't always act like it. Maybe someone had complained.

"I wanted to ask if you're a believer - a Christian," he continued.

Oh dear, this could go one of two ways. Either it would open the door for them to have an open conversation or her answer would earn her the same fiery reception it had from her boss. Kat took a deep breath and hoped it was the former. "I am. I guess I've always been, but I hadn't been a very good one until recently after my friend's death."

His eyes shot to hers, an intensity flowing out of them like she'd never seen before. "That's what I wanted to ask you about. Why does God let bad things happen?"

His question cut to her heart. It was one she had asked herself so many times, and she still wasn't sure she had the right answer.

"I mean I believe in God. When I look around at this world, I find it hard to believe someone didn't create it, but I'm having a hard time wanting to follow Him. If He is so good and loving, then why does He allow bad things to happen to people?"

Kat sent up a silent prayer for the right words and took a deep breath before answering. "Well, the first thing we have to remember is that God gives us free will. He hopes that we will make the right decisions, the ones that honor Him, but He gives us the choice to do otherwise. Some of our pain and hurt comes from making those poor decisions."

Brian nodded and drummed his fingers on the desk. "I understand that, but I'm talking about other things, things not based on our choices. For instance, there was a fighter who trained here, who served in the military, and who has a young daughter he adores. He's not even twenty-four, and I just found out he has a rare form of cancer and probably won't see the end of the year. And last Christmas, my dog died on Christmas Day with my whole family watching. Maybe that sounds silly, but we loved that dog, and his death was unexpected. Why does God allow those things to happen?"

Wow, he certainly knew how to cut right to the point. Kat wished she had asked Micah that question because she certainly didn't have the answer. Perhaps Micah would have more knowledge on the subject than she did. If she ever saw him again, it would be her first question. "Have you read the Bible, Brian?"

A look of chagrin covered his face, and his gaze dropped to his hands. "Some, but probably not as much as I should."

"Me neither, but I'm thinking about the book of Job. Do you know the story?"

"Is that the guy who had all the bad things happen to him?"

Kat nodded. "It is. See, God isn't the only supernatural being in this world. There are also angels and demons and Satan. The Bible says that in the new heaven, there will be no more pain and suffering because Satan and the demons will be thrown into the lake of fire, but until then, I believe these bad things are Satan's hands. He is crafty and cunning, and he tries to separate us from God any way he can. If the death of your dog and your fighter getting sick has caused you to doubt God, then he has succeeded."

Brian ran his hand across his chin, the stubble scraping against his hand and making a soft scratching sound. "I guess I never thought about it like that, but why allow Satan to influence us at all?"

"Because God wants to know we choose Him because we want to. If everything were rosy all the time, do you think people would come to God or would they forget about Him and settle into complacency?"

The squeak of un-oiled metal filled the air as Brian leaned back in his chair. He folded his arms across his chest and inhaled deeply. Kat wished she could see what was going through his mind, but she knew he had to be working over her response - mulling it over.

Suddenly the light behind him grew brighter. Kat resisted the urge to shield her eyes but was forced to turn her head. She hoped he wouldn't notice and ask why. Sharing her faith was one thing, but explaining to people that she saw angels was a whole other issue. As quickly as the light had grown bright, it dimmed. Not gone, but definitely not as bright as before.

"Thank you, Kat. You've opened my eyes to things I hadn't thought of before. I think I can finally start praying again."

Was that why his light had dimmed? Had he made the

ultimate decision? Or had he just gotten a step closer? Would his light disappear when he actually accepted? Again she wished Micah had given her more of a road map; she felt like she was navigating in the dark. "You're welcome."

As the silence stretched out between them, Kat knew that was her cue that the conversation was over. For now at least. "Well, I guess I'm going to go get changed for class," she said as she stood and threw her bag over her shoulder.

He glanced up at the clock. "Yep, it's about that time. Thanks again, Kat."

She nodded and continued to the locker room. Could she count that as a win? Micah had said the angels were protecting those who were close to making a decision, so maybe they left to protect someone else after the decision was made. Or maybe they were watching over several people and the brightness determined the amount of attention they needed. Maybe Brian's light had faded because he needed less attention now. There was just so much she still didn't know, and it weighed on her.

Raven stared at the clock and willed her boss to speak faster. If they didn't finish this meeting soon, she would miss the four o'clock class at the gym. It was her favorite hour to go, and missing it always threw her routine off. Plus, she got cranky when she was forced to skip a workout.

"Are there any questions?"

Finally. That was usually the line said right before the meeting ended. Raven silently willed everyone in the room to keep their mouths shut. Most of her co-workers were like herself - quiet and focused on doing the job and going home - but a few of them were overachievers and occasionally they would highjack meetings with their inane questions for an additional half an hour or more.

Her eyes found Betty, the worst offender, and she glared at the woman. If her hand went into the air, Raven just might lose it on her. Betty's arm twitched as if it was going to lift, and then she turned slightly and her eyes met Raven's. All color faded from her face, and her hands dropped to her lap.

"Okay, you're all dismissed then. Have a good night, and I'll see you tomorrow."

Yes. Raven pushed back her chair and grabbed her bag. A glance at her watch revealed she'd have just enough time to make class if traffic was light, but before she reached the doorway, a chill raced down her spine. Someone was watching her. Again. She turned to see who it was and nearly screamed. Black shadows flitted around the room. Though formless and faceless, they terrified her nonetheless, and her hand flew to her mouth.

"Raven, you okay?"

She blinked and the shapes were gone.

"Raven?"

Raven looked at the hand on her arm and up to the face of the man who owned it. Justin. She thought his name was Justin. He wasn't her type, so she hadn't bothered to commit his name to memory but that felt right. "What?"

He dropped his hand from her arm, but the concern didn't leave his eyes. "Are you okay? You looked like you'd seen a ghost there for a minute."

Had she seen a ghost? She wasn't sure she believed in them, but everything she'd ever seen or read depicted them as white shapes, not black. So, what had she seen? Probably nothing. More than likely, she was hallucinating from lack of sleep. Perhaps she needed to up the dose of her sleeping pills so she could finally get some decent rest. "I'm fine," she said when she realized she hadn't answered Justin's question. "Just thought I saw something, but it was nothing."

"Okay, if you're sure." He did not look convinced, but she knew he wouldn't press it. That was one of the benefits of her abrasive nature. She kept people far enough away that they might show concern, but they certainly weren't going to waste any sleep over her welfare.

"I'm sure." She tightened her grip on her bag and looked behind her one last time. No dark shapes, but she had to get a decent night's sleep tonight before she lost her mind.

She hurried out of the building and to her car, throwing her bag on the seat beside her and firing up the engine in one swift motion.

Raven pulled into the gym parking lot right at four o'clock. She hated being late, but thankfully there was always a few minutes of warm up. Loosening muscles before working out was important and she hated missing the stretching, but as long as she made it to class, that was all that mattered. Hitting things was her release, her way to channel the anger that continually coursed through her veins

"Raven, you in?" Brian asked her as she passed his desk.

"Yeah, sorry, work ran late. Give me five minutes to get changed."

He nodded and Raven continued to the locker room. Her eyes narrowed as she passed Kat running around the bags. The girl offered her a tentative smile, but Raven was in no mood.

"Cutting it close today, are we?" Jason stood at the locker room door, a teasing smile on his face.

"Yeah, but I'm here." She stepped close enough to touch him and let her arm brush against his, enjoying the way his gaze dropped to the collision of skin. "See you in a minute." She wiggled her eyebrows suggestively at him before continuing into the small locker room.

Once inside the stall, she pulled her work clothes off and quickly donned her workout gear. Then she grabbed her wraps, gloves, and hair tie and rejoined the main room. She had just finished placing the last clip in her hair to secure her dark locks when another dark shape flew across the room. A small scream escaped her mouth as she turned to see the shape hover near Jason and then disappear.

"Are you okay?"

Jordan turned to see Kat staring intently at her. Though she wasn't sure she was okay, Kat was the last person she wanted to talk to about this. "I'm fine." She grabbed her gloves and wraps and walked away from Kat before she could ask any further questions, but she was clearly *not* okay.

7

WEDNESDAY NIGHT

"So, how are things on the sharing front?" Patrick asked as he helped set the table for dinner. Patrick had been married to Stella, and though he and Kat hadn't been close before Stella's death, they had grown close since. He and Maddie, his five year old daughter, had come over to spend some time with Kat and Jordan. Kat was glad because Jordan had come home even more distracted today. Kat would have to talk with her later to see if the vision of the baby had gotten worse. For now, she was keeping Maddie busy with dolls or dress up or whatever else Maddie was into this week. Her tastes seemed to change daily.

Kat sighed in frustration as she placed the plate of chicken in the middle of the table. "Well, I had one break-through today with the owner of the gym. At least I think I did. He had a light and after we talked, the light dimmed. Of course, I have no idea if that means he became a believer or if his angel just disappeared, but at least it's something different. I wish Micah had given me more information."

"You haven't seen him again?" Patrick put the plate down and adjusted it until it was at the exact middle of the placemat. Kat had almost forgotten how OCD he was about certain things.

"No. I mean I'm glad he's not showing up in public anymore. Seeing lights is bad enough, I don't need any more people thinking I'm crazy and talking to myself. That already got me in trouble with work." Though she didn't want to see him in public, she still wished he would show up here or in her car. Somewhere so she could ask him all her questions.

"Still on suspension then?"

"Yep." Kat blew out a frustrated breath. "No sign of it lifting soon either."

Patrick placed the silverware on either side of the plate like sentinels guarding a treasure. "And how about Raven? How is that going?"

Kat's sigh this time was loud and exasperated. "It isn't. She still acts like I'm the enemy. She won't talk to me, but there's something going on with her. She's seeing something."

"How do you know?"

The memory of the moment at the gym when terror filled Raven's voice, and her eyes had been focused on something across the room that no one else could see flooded Kat's mind. "I saw her react to something. It scared her, but I couldn't see it and no one else could either from what I gathered. She denied it though when I asked her about it."

He moved to the next setting and began the routine all over again. "You think she's seeing angels like you are?"

Kat bit the inside of her lip. She supposed it was possible; she had been scared when she had first seen the lights before she knew what they were, but the terror in Raven's eyes had felt different. Like what she was seeing wasn't light at all, but dark. "I don't know. Do you think it's possible she's seeing demons? Do you think they could really be around us?" A shiver raced down her spine at the thought. She was fairly certain the Bible said something about demons and angels being around all the time, but for some reason, the thought gave her chills.

Patrick looked up at Kat and shook his head. "I don't know. A month ago, I would have said that sounded crazy, but now?" He shrugged and dropped his gaze back to the plate, giving it one more nudge.

"If they are, it means I have to hurry. I see lights everywhere, Patrick. How am I supposed to talk to all of those people?"

He set down the last fork and knife and looked up at

her. "Maybe it's not about talking to all of them - just as many as you can."

"Yeah, but then what happens to the others?" Kat bit her lip as she thought about how to explain her thoughts. They'd been running through her brain for a week, but she hadn't said them out loud until now. "What happens to the ones we don't talk to? Are they lost then? And what about people in other cities, in other states? We're only two people and there are seven billion people in the world. How are we supposed to reach seven billion people?"

Patrick walked around the table and placed a hand on her arm. "Kat, do you really think God doesn't have people all around the world doing just what you're doing?"

She blinked at him. Was he saying that other people saw lights? Saw angels? That she wasn't the lone freak? Well, after the incident with Raven today, she was pretty sure she wasn't the lone freak, but could there be more? Her words came out slow and unsure. "You think there are more people like us?"

His kind eyes regarded her a little like they did Maddie when he had to explain something simple to her. "How could there not be? You said yourself that there are seven billion people on this earth. There's no way you and Jordan could reach them all, and we know God is a loving God who wants everyone to choose Him. There are probably hundreds of people like you and Jordan out there."

Kat supposed it was possible. It certainly made sense,

but if there were others like her, where were they? She wanted to meet them. Why couldn't Micah have left more instructions, more guidance? "You're probably right. So, I guess I shouldn't worry so much about the ones I can't talk to?" Though that didn't remove her burden completely, it did ease it a little.

"I have to believe someone else will talk with them if you are unable. I think the thing to do is focus on talking to as many as you can in the time we have left."

The time they had left. It felt so foreign. She'd heard about the rapture growing up, but it had just been a story then - a fairy tale. Now, here it was looming before her - or, at least, that was the assumption. God was still in control of the timing, so her "almost here" might still be years for Him. But she didn't think so. Micah had seemed urgent in his request, and suddenly all the things she had wanted to do flashed in front of her eyes.

Marriage. She had wanted to wait until she was settled in her career, but she had wanted to get married. And kids. Maddie was amazing, but Maddie wasn't her child - her flesh and blood. She had wanted to experience carrying a child, rocking them, seeing the unconditional love in their eyes. Now that might never happen and the sadness of it weighed on her. She knew seeing Jesus was more important - the only thing that mattered. And probably when she got to heaven she wouldn't be sad about not having her own baby, but that didn't make the feelings any less real right now.

As if reading her mind, Patrick squeezed her arm. "Kat, are you okay?"

She shook her head, her throat choked with emotions at the moment. Emotions at her responsibility. Emotions at what she might be losing. Emotions at how much time she had wasted worrying about things that didn't matter now. She thought back to all the dates she had turned down in college, so she could study. Had one of them been her soul mate? Could she have had her career and marriage too if she'd been more open? It was all too much to bear. "I'm not sure I am." Her words were barely more than a whisper, but they were all she could force past the knot in her throat.

"It's okay, Kat. You have every right to be scared and worried, but God has this under control. Do you know how you eat an elephant?"

Kat's eyes flicked to his. An elephant? What was he talking about? "People don't eat elephants." Actually, she wasn't sure of that. Somewhere they probably did, but what did that have to do with their discussion?

Patrick grinned, and his shoulders shook with a silent chuckle. "You always were literal, Kat. No, you eat an elephant one bite at a time."

Kat narrowed her eyes at him. Was he really making a

joke right now? She was confessing her soul and he was joking?

"I think your situation is like that. Think of these people as the elephant. You can't reach all of them at once, but you can reach one at a time, and slowly they will form the whole elephant. One step at a time. Those people you do reach will then talk to someone else - the butterfly effect in all its glory."

This was what Stella had seen in him. As he stared at her with his sincere, earnest eyes, Kat knew that this was the part of him that had won Stella's heart. And though she would never be thankful for Stella's death, she was glad to have gotten to know him better, and she was certainly grateful she had a friend like him in her corner.

She took a deep breath and nodded. Right. Baby steps. "Okay, no more worrying about what I can't control. I'll just worry about what I can. That's certainly enough worry on its own."

He flashed her a smile and squeezed her arm before removing his hand and turning back to the table. "That a girl, and one thing we can control right now is dinnertime, right?"

Kat felt a smile tug at her lips. "Indeed. Want to round up the girls?"

"It would be my pleasure."

Jordan stared at the open Bible on her lap, but she wasn't reading it. Not really. Every time her eyes skimmed the verse, her mind would think back over the day instead of focus on the words. There had been no visions today. None. For the first time in months, her head had been silent, still, and it felt wrong.

"You want to tell me what's going on with you?" Kat handed her a mug of tea before setting her own mug on the end table and sitting in the recliner a few feet away. She tucked her feet, clad in pink polka dot socks, under her legs and fixed Jordan with a knowing stare.

"I wish I knew." Jordan picked up the mug and watched the tiny clouds of steam rise and dance in the air. "I had no visions today."

"And that's bad because?" Kat was trying hard to understand; Jordan could see it on her face, but how did you explain the deafening silence to someone who didn't see movies in their head?

"It's bad because I haven't not had a vision in months. Every morning, it's like my own private movie theater in my head. I see the women who will come into the clinic that day. I see what they are hiding or running from, and I see how it will end up if they don't change course. Every day. Like clockwork. Until this morning."

The light of recognition dawned on Kat's face. "Are you worried you may have lost your gift?"

Jordan chuckled. Though she enjoyed helping people, seeing all their dirty laundry and confronting them about it didn't really feel like a gift. Still, it had been happening so long, it now felt like a part of her. "I don't know if worry is the right word, but I feel like a piece of me is missing. It would be like if you stopped seeing lights all of a sudden. Only I've been having visions a lot longer."

Kat picked up her mug and took a slow sip. "Okay, I can see how that would be stressful, but maybe it's just the situation, Jordan. We've been given a big job and maybe the stress is affecting your visions. I was just telling Patrick at dinner how worried I was about the people I couldn't talk to. Maybe you're feeling something similar."

Jordan wanted to believe that was all it was. She'd definitely been stressed, but a part of her knew that wasn't the whole issue. "I think mine might be something more."

"Something more? What do you mean?" Concern was etched in Kat's furrowed brow and compassionate eyes.

"I mean those visions about the baby, and I keep thinking about my son. Working with all these pregnant women has always been a reminder, but now that I know the end is coming soon, I can't get him out of my head. I think I need to go back and see him one last time."

"Do you know who adopted him?"

Jordan took a sip of her tea, enjoying the warmth it spread through her body. She hadn't realized she was so cold. "Yes, I did an open adoption. I wanted him to be able to find me later if he had questions or if he wanted to have a relationship."

"So, why don't you go back and see him?"

Jordan let the words bounce around in her head before answering. "I want to, but is it what I'm supposed to do? Didn't Micah say I was supposed to stay here and help you?"

Kat pursed her lips and Jordan knew she was thinking back to the encounter. "He said we were to work together, but I don't think that meant we had to be in the same town. Besides, if you aren't having visions, I'm not sure you could help much. I need a way to get Raven to listen to me, but you know her even less than I do."

Though Jordan was sure Kat hadn't meant them that way, the words felt like a dagger to her heart. She wasn't being useful because she was too focused on something else. "I'm so sorry, Kat. I feel like I'm letting you down."

Kat set her mug down and crossed to sit next to Jordan. "You're not letting anyone down, and what if you're supposed to save that baby? Maybe when you take care of this, your visions will come back."

Emotion burned the back of Jordan's throat, and she sniffed to keep the tears at bay. "Do you think so? I've tried to just forget about him, but I can't."

"I'm almost sure of it. You do what you need to do, and we'll figure out where to go from there."

Kat draped an arm around Jordan's shoulders, and

Jordan let herself sink into the warm embrace. Maybe Kat was right. Maybe once she returned to Texas and saw her son, her visions would return and she could continue to help Kat. All she could do was hope and pray.

Raven shivered and pulled the blanket tighter around her shoulders. Why was she so cold? She crossed to the thermostat to turn it up a few degrees, but the temperature read seventy-three. Not cold. So what was going on?

"Raven." The voice was soft and it drew her name out making each syllable feel even longer.

Raven whirled around, but there was no one in the room with her. "Who's there?"

The light sound of laughter came back to her, just a whisper in the air, but that was enough for Raven. She needed to get out of here. The clock read eight. Though she'd already worked out today, perhaps she could do another hour. Maybe sweat and physical exhaustion would block out whatever was going on with her. Even if they didn't, being around other people would calm her nerves. Her apartment was too quiet, and her mind was playing tricks on her for sure.

She hurried toward her bedroom to grab her gym bag, but the cold sensation didn't leave as she entered her room. Instead, it felt like it followed her, and she could swear she felt eyes on her as she grabbed a new set of workout clothes and shoved them in her bag. She held her breath, ears straining for some sound - a footfall, a breath, a creak of the floor. But nothing more came.

Of course nothing came. She was alone in the apartment. Stressed, obviously which was why she thought she was hearing things, but alone. Raven pulled back her shoulders, hefted her bag onto her shoulders, and forced her eyes to stay on the path in front of her as she exited the apartment.

When the front door closed behind her, the chill finally left her body. What had happened in there? It made no sense, but there had to be a reasonable explanation for it. Raven didn't believe in anything she couldn't see or touch, so even though she briefly flirted with the idea of something supernatural, she dismissed it. Her mind playing tricks on her due to lack of sleep and stress made much more sense.

Raven continued to convince herself of that reasoning all the way to the gym, but she couldn't shake the feeling that maybe there was more to it than lack of sleep.

8

THURSDAY

Raven stared down at the empty clothing in her hands. A moment ago, a child had filled them, but now there was nothing. Screams flooded the air around her, and she looked up to see other women staring, as she did, down at nothing.

"Gemma? Has anyone seen Gemma?" "Calvin? Calvin, where are you?" The shouts of names grew on top of one another creating a cacophonous noise until they drowned each other out.

Raven dropped the clothing and focused on the car - the car that had burst through the front glass windows of the gym. She limped over to the driver's side. The man inside had blood streaming down one side of his face, and his lips mumbled something, but she could not understand it.

With a gasp, the image faded, and she sat up and looked around the dark room. The unfamiliar dark room. This wasn't her bedroom - there were no black curtains, no landscape photos, so where was she? And then it came back to her. Jason, after hearing her story the night before, had offered his couch and Raven had taken him up on it not wanting to return home.

She clicked the button on her smartwatch to illuminate the screen. Four-thirty - too early, but like the previous nights, she wasn't sure she was getting any more sleep tonight. She might as well go in to work early to catch up on what she had missed due to the meeting yesterday.

Raven scribbled a quick note to Jason to explain where she'd gone before heading to the bathroom to catch a quick shower. He'd offered it to her last night and even left a towel out for her, but she'd been too tired to take it then. She would enjoy the warmth now, though she wished she had another pair of clothes with her. Perhaps, she could stop by her place just long enough to grab something. The thought of returning home still filled her with dread, but she couldn't show up to work in yesterday's clothing. That would create gossip she didn't want or need.

She peeled off her clothes and stepped into the warm shower. His water pressure wasn't as good as hers, but the effect was the same. The heat from the water poured into her body, waking her up and dispelling the last remnants of darkness. Maybe she should try a shower before bed or warm milk. Something to calm her brain before she fell asleep so that she could avoid these dreams.

What had that dream even been? A child disappearing. A car crashing through her gym. The gym was on a main road, but it sat a good twenty feet from the road and up a curb. A car would have to be going pretty quickly to come barreling in the front of the gym like that.

She turned the water off and dried off before pulling on her clothes again and sneaking out of the house. Darkness still coated the landscape like a thick black ink, and Raven's heart steadily increased its pace. What if someone was hiding in the shadows? What if the dark shapes were there watching her, just waiting for the perfect time to attack?

Her eyes closed for the briefest of seconds. She had to get a hold of herself. Only crazy people thought they saw dark shapes or imagined people lurking in the shadows, and she was not crazy.

She repeated that mantra as she drove to her apartment, but it didn't slow her heart rate down any as she parked her Jeep and turned off the engine. What if someone had gotten inside while she was gone? Had she even remembered to lock the door in her haste to leave the night before?

Ten minutes. She just needed ten minutes to grab some clothes. It was such a short amount of time, but her heart refused to understand. Her feet dragged on the pavement as she forced herself toward her front door.

The locked handle gave her a slight reprieve. At least no one had gotten in this way. She unlocked the door and pushed it open, letting the little light from outside spill into the living room. Nothing appeared to move, and the laughter she had heard the night before was silent now. Imagination. That's all it had been.

Her brain repeated that message as she flicked on every light on the way to her bedroom. Yes, just her imagination. Perhaps with an imagination like hers, she should leave coding and write books. If she could scare herself this much, what could she do to readers?

Raven's shoulders slowly relaxed as she changed out of the old clothes and into a new outfit. How silly she'd been to not want to come home last night. There was nothing here, nothing to worry about. This was her apartment, her refuge. She was safe here.

She checked her hair and makeup in the bathroom mirror before heading out, but though she had almost convinced herself of her safety, she did not glance at anything other than her reflection in the mirror. Nor did she let her eyes wander as she made her way back to the front door, locked it behind her, and continued to the car.

Forty-five minutes later, Raven entered the building where she worked. The lobby lights were on, but the place felt cold and empty. The first shift began at seven, so other than the night watchman, there was no one else in the building. She liked it that way, enjoyed the quiet. Normally. Today, however, she wondered if the quiet would allow her mind to play more tricks on her, to make her think she was seeing things that weren't there.

She waved to the watchman who sat behind the receptionist desk on her way to "the maze." It wasn't really a maze, but the rows and rows of cubicles always made her feel as if she were in one. It was not her ideal workstation, but thankfully her cubicle was near the back and away from most of the traffic.

She dropped her purse under the desktop and powered on the computer. Might as well catch up on the email first. The promotion she had put in for was supposed to be announced any day, and she would really enjoy an actual office with walls where she could block out the annoying conversations that often flowed around her.

A moment later, her screen glowed, and her computer hummed softly. Raven clicked to the email server and waited for it to load. There it was - the email announcing the promotee - at the top of her inbox. She clicked the email and felt her jaw drop. Frustration surged within her. She'd been passed over again? This job wasn't rocket science, and she'd been doing it for the last year, so why did everyone around her keep getting the promotion she deserved?

She knew her attitude could be abrasive at times -

people had been kind enough to tell her that on more than one occasion - but she could also turn the charm up when she wanted. Besides, she worked in coding. She didn't need to be nice to people; she just needed to be able to write and repair programs. And she could. She was good at it.

Her eyes fell to the bottom of the email where the lucky recipient was listed. Cindy Berkowitz? Really? Cindy wasn't bad at her job, but she was annoying. Chipper and smiley like Kat. The sunshine of the department. Probably a Christian too if the cross she wore on her neck was any indication. Irritation rose in Raven at the thought of Kat again, and she slammed her hands on the desk.

Cindy had stolen her job; now Kat was stealing her gym. True, Jason had let her stay the night last night, but he'd seemed immune to her charms, and though he hadn't, Raven had sensed he wanted to talk about Kat. She had to find a way to stop her.

Movement in the corner of her eye grabbed her attention, and Raven looked up to see a shadow flit across her computer screen. Not again. Her head whipped behind her, but there was no one there. Just rows of empty cubicles. Nothing else moved in the large room.

What was going on? She'd been seeing way too many of these dark shapes to dismiss them as hallucinations from lack of sleep, and she was getting dangerously close to overdosing on sleeping pills if she kept upping the dosage. Maybe Kat was a witch and had cursed her. Could that really happen? Raven shook her head. She'd been watching too many Supernatural reruns. That kind of thing didn't happen in real life. Right? Just to be sure, she decided to call out and see if anyone or anything responded.

"Hello?" As her voice echoed in the room, she thought of every horror movie she had ever watched. How many times had she yelled at the girl on TV not to call out, but to run, yet here she was doing the same thing.

Raven stood up and scanned the room more closely. She hated the cubicles. Not only did they make her feel like a mouse in a trap, but someone could easily be hiding in one now and without peeking over every wall, she would never know it.

"Is anyone there?" Silence blanketed the room as her voice stilled, almost like that eerie quiet after a snowfall, but this wasn't comforting like the sight of the delicate white flakes. No, this felt quite different. Chilling, even. The hairs on her arm and the back of her neck lifted as if coaxed upward by some unseen hand, and that was enough for Raven. There might not be anything physical in the room, but something was definitely off.

Suddenly her phone began ringing. Even though her ring tone was a song and not a shrill ringing, the sudden sound of it breaking the silence made her jump. She snatched it out of her pocket, hitting the call button as she did. "Hello?" Her voice sounded breathy and scared, and her eyes continued to scan the room as she waited for the voice on the other end to speak.

"Raven Ryder?" The voice was deep and masculine and not one she recognized.

"You tell me. You called my phone."

"I need you to come to my office. It is imperative we speak."

His office? Who was this and why was he calling on her cell instead of the office phone? In fact, why was he even in the office this early? She was only here because of the nightmares and the need to be doing something besides sitting around and jumping at shadows. It was possible he had work to do or perhaps, like her, he enjoyed the silence, but she'd never seen a boss here this early before.

"Who is this?" She hated how shaky her voice sounded, how weak.

"Room 144. If you value your job, you will be here in under ten minutes."

Raven was about to argue with the mysterious voice when the phone went dead in her ear. "Hello?" She knew the word was useless at this point, but it slipped past her lips anyway. Great. Now what did she do? She had no idea who had been on the phone, but he was creepy. However, the black shapes and whatever was in the room with her here might be even creepier. With a resigned sigh, she jammed her phone back into her pocket, grabbed her bag from under the desk, and hurried out of the cubicle maze. Though she felt eyes on her as she walked, she did not turn around. The fear of what she might see kept her jaw clenched and her gaze firmly in front of her.

The tense feeling ebbed as she stepped into the lobby. Perhaps it was the openness of the room or the early morning sunlight now filtering in the large windows that dispelled the fear. She honestly didn't care. As long as it was gone.

She turned left to exit the building but stopped. The elevator called to her like a silent beacon. What if the guy was real? What if he was one of her bosses? She couldn't afford to lose this job. Her eyes flicked to the receptionist desk. She could ask the watchman if anyone else was in the building, but the desk was empty. He must have run to the bathroom or to grab a bite of food. Of course, the one time she needed him and he wasn't at his post.

Raven bit her lip as indecision held her rooted to the spot. Her eyes glanced from one door to the other. Finally, she shook her head and turned toward the elevator. She hoped she wasn't making the biggest mistake of her life.

The silver doors opened, reminding Raven of mechanical jaws. She had to stop watching so many horror shows. Her finger trembled slightly as she pressed the circular number one, but she forced herself not to jump when they slid shut and the car began to move.

When they opened again, she scanned the area for signs. She'd only been on the first floor once - when she first got hired. The ground level of the building contained the lobby, the cubicle maze where she worked, the kitchen and break area, and bathrooms, so she rarely had cause to go anywhere else. The floor above contained the offices, of which Raven had only been in two - her immediate boss' office for the interview and the human resource office to fill out the necessary paperwork. Raven had no idea what was on the other floors as she'd never felt the need to investigate.

According to the sign, room 144 lay to the right. Raven hadn't even known there were that many offices on this floor - it didn't seem that large - but maybe they were numbered oddly. Her mother's street had been that way, numbered every third number instead of every number.

When she reached the designated room, she raised her hand to knock, but before her hand even touched the door, a voice called out. "Come in."

Her hand froze in the air. How had he known she was out here? Perhaps this wasn't safe after all. No one even knew where she was. This guy could be some crazy man who snuck in and planned to gut her or worse, but if it were some random guy, how would he have known her cell number. Stupid, stupid, stupid played over in her mind, but she pushed the door open anyway.

The office wasn't large, nor was it opulent. In fact, it

had a bare-bones feel to it. No pictures or plaques adorned the walls, and they were devoid of color. In fact, the only color in the room was on the man himself. His jacket was dark, but his shirt was a vivid blue, accentuated even more by the blandness of the room.

"Hello, Raven, I'm Micah. Nice to meet you."

He did not stand which only unnerved Raven more. She'd never seen this man before, and something about him seemed off, but she couldn't place what it was. "Am I in trouble?" She hated beating around the bush - better to jump right in and find out what they had on her. It was obviously something because she couldn't imagine why she would be called here if it wasn't.

A flicker of something flashed in his eyes before his stoic demeanor took over again. "Your job is not in jeopardy."

She blinked at him. That hadn't been her question.

"You are here because you saw something."

"I saw something?" Raven made it her point to see nothing, hear nothing. She avoided office gossip like the plague. What television show aired the night before or who was dating whom did not matter to her, and she could not force herself to engage in idle chatter.

"At the meeting yesterday. I was informed you behaved oddly. Your superiors decided that perhaps a few counseling sessions could help." He spread his hands out. "I am that counselor."

A counselor? Was he crazy? She wasn't telling anyone about the black shapes, least of all this guy whom she didn't know from Adam and who spoke like a robot. "Yeah, thanks for the offer, but I'm all good. I was just tired. Burning the midnight oil and all that."

His head tilted slightly and his forehead furrowed as if he didn't understand her metaphor. "It is not a request. You have been assigned sessions with me in order to retain your job. We can begin the first one now."

Raven scanned the room for cameras. This had to be a joke though she could think of no one who would pull such a joke on her. No one here knew her well enough or cared enough about her to pull a joke. "You're saying if I don't talk to you, then I'm fired?"

He shrugged. "I believe you will find me easy to talk to."

As if compelled by his words, Raven suddenly found herself wanting to talk to him. She sat down in the chair across from him, barely noticing it was a folding chair and not like the rest of the furniture in the building. She placed her arms on the desk - oddly devoid of any clutter, pictures, or writing utensils - and stared at him. "I've been seeing shapes. Black shapes." Even as the words left her mouth, she couldn't believe she was saying them aloud to him, but she seemed unable to stop. It was as if her mouth was under some kind of spell.

Micah folded his hands together and nodded. "And do these shapes have form? Do they have faces?"

"Faces?" She leaned back in the chair. Was he crazy? "No, they don't have faces. They're just shadows - probably just my mind playing tricks on me, but every time I see them, I feel as if someone is watching me."

"And have you told anyone else of these shapes?"

Did he think she was an idiot? Talking about black shapes that didn't exist would most likely get her fired and labeled as crazy. Neither of those things was high on her to-do list. "No, I haven't told anyone. I'm not insane." However, she was beginning to have her doubts about him. He hadn't even flinched when she told him about the shapes, just kept up with that same robotically calm demeanor.

"It may be important to talk to someone about what you are seeing at some point. For now, you can continue to share your concerns with me. Now, shall we talk about your stepfather?"

Her stepfather? How did he know anything about her stepfather? It wasn't like that was in her file. Was he trying to psychoanalyze her? "I'm sorry, is this counseling or therapy?"

His steely eyes bore into hers. "Is there a difference?"

"Yeah, there is. Counseling can be mandated by my employers but it would only pertain to whatever was affecting my work. Therapy cannot be mandated by my employers and that is where talking about my stepfather would fall. You said I had to attend these sessions. Fine, but I'll only talk about things that might affect my work and my stepfather is not one of them."

Again his head cocked like a parrot when it listened to someone speak. "You do not believe that what your stepfather put you through when you were young affects your work now?"

Okay, this had just gone from weird to downright creepy. No one here knew about her stepfather. In fact, no one other than her mother knew, and her mother was usually too stoned to care. "I don't know who you are, but this counseling session is over." Raven stood and began walking toward the door, but before she reached it, Micah's voice froze her steps.

"The time is short, Raven Ryder. You need to come to grips with your past, so that you can affect your future. The fate of many lay with you."

She turned to face him. "I've made peace with my past, and the only person's fate that I have control over is my own."

His lips curled into a tight smile. "We shall discuss more next time, Raven. I believe your curiosity will get the better of you."

Raven doubted that, but even as she left room 144, she found herself wondering what he had meant about her future. What did he know that she didn't? And why did it seem as if he thought someone else knew as well?

Kat held her hand up as a bright light illuminated the locker room. Raven. It had to be. The angel on her shoulder was brighter than most, but Kat wasn't ready to talk to Raven yet. She still had no idea what to say. The girl had been shooting daggers her direction the whole class, and she'd brushed off Kat's efforts to reach out to her yesterday. Something had obviously happened to Raven, but she seemed intent on keeping it to herself. So, Kat had done her best to avoid her, but the locker room was small and there were not many places to hide.

"Hey, Raven," Kat said, pasting a bright smile on her face as she pulled her watch out of her bag to put it back on her wrist. It was painful to wear her watch with boxing gloves on, but she felt so naked without it that it was the first thing she put on after every class. "Are you okay?"

"Why do you care?" Raven asked as she dropped her gloves in her bag.

Kat sighed and sent up a silent prayer for help. What could she say to get Raven to open up to her? To allow Kat to at least say the words she needed to? She aimed for a nonchalant tone, adding a shrug with her words. "What can

I say? I'm a caring person, and I know you saw something yesterday."

Raven's posture stiffened, and her eyes took on a cold, steely glare. "I don't know what you're talking about. I saw nothing other than you throwing yourself at Jason. Or is it Jon this week?"

Kat bristled at Raven's insinuation. She had no desire to date any of the men here. They all seemed nice enough, but Micah had made it clear that Kat's mission came first. "You've got it all wrong, Raven. I'm not here to hook up with anyone, and I heard you scream. I know you saw something. Tell me what you saw."

Raven ignored the last question, but her eyes roamed Kat's body from head to toe with a critical gaze as she began unwrapping her wrists. "Then why are you here? I mean, no offense, but you don't look like you could take anyone in a fight. You look...weak."

Kat mashed her lips together to keep the hateful words simmering in her brain from pouring out of her mouth. Raven was lost, hurting. She needed to remember that. But it was hard. So hard. Especially with her spouting off about things she couldn't understand.

"I came because I needed a place to focus my anger. My best friend died recently, and I was having trouble dealing with it. I met Jason at the bar he works at one night, and he recommended this place, this workout. So, I didn't come here to hook up with him or anyone else. I came here to channel my anger, so I didn't explode." Kat took a moment to take a calming breath. "Why do you hate me so much anyway, Raven? You don't even know me."

Raven scoffed and tossed her wraps into her bag. "I don't have to know you. I've known enough people like you. You play this sweet, innocent card until people trust you, and then you reveal your true colors and shove the knife in."

Kat shook her head softly. She could only imagine what lay in Raven's past to make her so wary. "What happened to you, Raven? What happened to make you so hard?"

"Nothing happened to me. I'm too strong to let anything happen to me, but I've seen it plenty of times." Raven pulled on her zipper with an angry yank and then picked up her bag. "You should just do yourself a favor and find another gym. You're not welcome here."

Kat stood and slung her bag over her shoulder. "I can't do that, Raven." Oh, how she wished she could. She was beginning to wonder if talking to Raven was even possible.

"Why not?"

"Because I'm not done yet."

Raven's brows pulled together, and she looked at Kat as if she were crazy. "Done? With what? Training? You're never done. It's a lifestyle, not some crazy fad."

Kat shook her head. She didn't want to say anymore. Raven already thought she was loony, but she could feel the gentle pressure on her heart, urging her to continue. "No, not with training. With you."

"With me?" Raven's eyes snapped up to lock with Kat's. "What do you want with me? I don't swing that way if that's what you're after."

"What?" Kat shook her head as a wave of embarrassment swirled in her stomach. "No, it's not like that. I'm supposed to talk to you."

Raven popped out her hip and pursed her lips. "Talk to me? About what?"

Kat inhaled deeply. Raven was probably about to think she was even crazier, but she had to try. "About what you saw out there. About your future."

Raven's body tensed, and her jaw clenched before a loud, hoarse laugh spilled out of her full lips. "My future?" She shook her head, and Kat couldn't help but notice that she had once again skirted the issue of what she'd seen. "That's ripe. What are you some kind of fortune teller?"

Yep. This was going about as good as Kat had expected. "No, not a fortune teller. Not exactly anyway."

Raven's eyes narrowed and her posture shifted. Every muscle in her body appeared to tense as she glared at Kat. "Oh, no, you're one of those religious nuts, aren't you? You here to tell me all about Jesus and how my soul is in danger?"

Kat cringed at Raven's tone and gripped her bag tighter. "It's not like that."

"Yeah, okay." Raven rolled her eyes and hiked her bag up higher on her shoulder. "I think I'll pass. I'm maxed out on crazy."

"Raven, wait." But it was too late. Raven had already turned and walked out of the room. Kat could chase her, but what would be the point? Her job was hard enough but now with Raven's admission of hatred for believers. What was she supposed to do with that?

With a sigh, Kat waited another few seconds to make sure Raven was gone before exiting the locker room. She'd have to keep praying and hope God opened a door for her.

Raven glanced over her shoulder as she pushed open the side door to the gym. She needed to be sure Kat wasn't following her yet.

The five o'clock class was just starting, so there was a stream of people standing between the bags and stretching in her sight line, but she did not see the dark-haired girl among them. Good. It would give her time to get to her car and wait for Kat to exit. She needed to know what the girl drove.

Unfortunately as it was summer, the sun still shone brightly overhead. Were it winter, it would already be dark by now and the shadows would conceal her, but no such luck. Plus, her car would be hot and steamy. Uncomfortable to sit in too long without cracked windows or the air conditioner on. Hopefully Kat wasn't too far behind her.

She yanked open the door of her Jeep and climbed inside, shutting her door just as the side door opened again on the building. With a hiss of frustration, she ducked down as far as she could while still maintaining a visual on the door.

Kat emerged a second later, and without glancing around, she walked to a blue Mini Cooper. At least she had good taste in cars. Raven had always wanted a Mini Cooper, but not one off the lot. She wanted to be able to order it to her specifications like they did in the movies. And there was a website where you could do that, but Raven would never be able to afford the price. She wondered what Kat did?

Was she an heiress like Paris Hilton or did she actually work for her money? If Raven had to wager a bet, she'd guess the latter. Kat seemed too earnest to be a stuck-up heiress. But there lay the quandary. If Kat was earnest and truthful, then did she know something about Raven's future? Or about the dark shapes Raven kept seeing? Should Raven at least let her talk before completely dismissing her as a quack?

No. She'd known too many hypocritical Christians in her time. Heck, her stepfather had been friends with one of the greeters at the church. That hadn't stopped him from taking a turn with Raven when she'd been offered up.

The Mini Cooper hummed to life, and Kat pulled out of the parking lot. Raven ducked down further in her seat until the Mini was out of sight. Then slowly she exhaled and sat up. Now, she knew what Kat drove. The questions was... what did she do about it?

Jordan stared at the text message from Jeremy, not believing her eyes. She'd met Jeremy on her flight from Texas to Washington a few weeks ago. He'd been like her guardian angel, easing her anxiety and helping her out in the crowded airport which had been odd because ever since the night of her rape, she'd had trouble trusting men. Heck, she'd had trouble passing them on the street without her heart hammering out of her chest and her palms turning into a sweaty mess. It was like she suspected every guy she passed might try to pull the same stunt - drug her, rape her, and then disappear. Jeremy, however, was different. He'd been planning to work with his father, so they had separated at the Seattle airport, but they'd kept in touch through text the last few weeks.

Last night, she had texted him about her plan to return to Texas though she hadn't mentioned why. Her son was still one of the many topics they had yet to discuss. They'd shared some personal information, both at the airport and in the time since. She knew a little about his caring family, he knew even less about her overbearing and critical mother, but her son, and the circumstances around his conception, was a topic she didn't share with many people. Only when it was required to convince people of her gift did she speak of him, and she hadn't even shared her gift with Jeremy. So, how odd that his text message stated that he was heading back to Texas as well. Was it possible they would meet again?

"When are you leaving?" Her fingers flew over the keys, but she didn't really think they would be lucky enough to be on the same flight again. What would be the odds? As she waited for the buzz of her phone to tell her that he had responded, she packed what little clothing she had brought with her back into her suitcase. How odd that God had sent her all the way out here to reach Kat and now it almost seemed as if He were sending her back. Couldn't He have used someone closer?

She knew His ways, like His timing, was not for her to question, but it was odd. Of course, it could be that this wasn't His way at all but her own selfish desires clouding her judgment, but she didn't think so. She'd spent most of the night praying about it after talking with Kat, and the only decision that gave her peace was going home.

The phone buzzed, and she snatched it up, swiping the screen as she did.

"Tomorrow morning. Eight a.m."

Jordan nearly dropped the phone. That was her flight

time as well. With shaky fingers, she tapped out her next message, "What flight?"

"United 762." This time the response was nearly instant as if he were waiting by the phone for her response.

United 762. Her flight. But how was that possible? She hadn't even planned on going back, yet somehow she was booked on the same flight as the one man she had connected with in the last year. Jordan didn't believe in coincidences, but she found this disconcerting. Who was Jeremy and what was his connection to her? She didn't want to text back, but it would be rude to leave his text unanswered. "Guess I'll see you tomorrow then." But did she want to? For the first time since meeting him, she found herself feeling a little afraid.

❧ 9 ❧

FRIDAY

The sound of the glass shattering echoed like tiny bells as the front windows exploded. Slivers of iridescent shards sprayed through the room as the front end of a car roared into the gym. The kids! Raven dashed toward the closest child. She couldn't save them all, but she could save one. Her arms circled the child, and she tugged, dragging the girl with her as she jumped out of the way. Screams and the echoes of groaning metal as it gave way thundered in her ears as she landed on her side.

Pain flared in her hip and licked greedily up and down her side like a ravenous lion. But she was safe. And the girl was safe. She glanced down to assess the girl's injuries and screamed. There was no girl, but in her arms she held the karate ghee the girl had been wearing. As if it were a snake, she dropped it and backed away. Where had the girl gone?

And then other screams joined Raven's. She looked up and realized women all around the gym were screaming; but they weren't screaming at the car, a silver Tesla that had come to a stop half way across the floor and now billowed smoke from beneath the hood. No, they were screaming as Raven had - with clothing clutched in their hands.

She looked around and realized there were no more children in the gym. Only adults. Where had the children gone?

"Is everybody okay?" Brian yelled from the side of the gym. He brushed shards of glass off his shirt as he surveyed the area.

"Where's my daughter?" "Where's my son?" The women's voices rose in a tumultuous cacophony as they yelled over each other for attention.

Raven assessed her injuries as she stood. Her ankle screamed in protest as she tried to put weight on it, and she leaned on a nearby bag for support. Sprained? More than likely. Her hip throbbed from the fall, and a few minor cuts dotted her arms and legs. She'd be sore, but she was okay. With slow, limping steps, she made her way over to the car. No one else seemed concerned about the driver at all, but she supposed that was to be expected with all the missing children.

"Are you hurt?" she asked when she reached the driver's side. His window was shattered, and his face lacerated. He blinked at her as if trying to bring her into focus.

"There was no one there."

"What? What do you mean?"

"In the car coming at me. I swerved to avoid hitting them, but there was no one there. How does a car drive itself?"

Raven gasped and shot up in bed. Her heart pounded in her chest as she looked around her darkened room. Shadows still blanketed the area; night had not yet surrendered to the day. She glanced at her alarm clock. The red numbers read 4:58. Not again. Why did she keep having this nightmare?

Children gone? Drivers vanished? Had she watched something crazy on television last night? No, she'd been too tired after her workout. Nor had she eaten anything crazy. Chicken and salad like always. There had been the weird meeting yesterday, but surely that wasn't the cause. He hadn't told her to meet him today. In fact, she didn't even know when their next appointment was which was a little odd. If counseling had been required, wouldn't he have sent her a calendar of meetings? Not that she wanted to meet with him, but she thought that was standard procedure.

Or was it Kat? She'd dismissed Kat's words as the

ramblings of a crazy woman, but when Raven combined that with Micah's words - it was a little harder to brush off. The last words they exchanged still fluttered around in her head like butterflies. Kat had said she knew something about Raven's future, but Raven hadn't believed her. However, now there were dark shapes appearing nearly every day, a crazy guy who claimed he was her counselor, and weird, vivid dreams. If Kat knew something about her future, then maybe it was time Raven found out what.

Kat stared at her computer screen as she thought of what to say next. The end was coming soon. She could feel it - see it in the increase of lights - but she hadn't accomplished her goal yet. Raven was an impenetrable wall. No chinks existed that she could find, and no matter how hard Kat tried, she could not get the girl to lower her defenses. Something terrible must have happened to her to cause her to hate the thought of God so much.

Kat understood hating God. After he'd taken her best friend, she'd been angry too, but then the lights had come. The lights and Jordan and Micah. While she might have been able to ignore Jordan and maybe even pretend the lights didn't exist, it was pretty impossible to ignore an angel. Especially when he unfurled his wings and showered her with a holy light like she'd never seen. She'd felt a little like Saul when he'd been blinded, but, like him, it had allowed her to see. Now, if she just knew how she could reach Raven.

"What are you doing?"

Kat looked up to see Jordan enter the kitchen, her suitcase rolling behind her. While Kat understood Jordan's need to return home, she was going to miss the girl. It had been nice having someone to talk to, especially someone who understood what she was going through.

"I'm typing up a manifesto, a guideline if you will."

Jordan's brow wrinkled in confusion. She grabbed a water from the fridge and then sat across from Kat at the kitchen table. "What's it for?"

Kat sighed. "It's mainly for Raven. I can't seem to reach her, but I think it will also be helpful for anyone else who won't believe us. I'm typing up what most people think will happen - that believers will disappear first and foremost. When we're gone, they're going to need to look somewhere. My hope is that I'll have planted enough seeds with Raven that when we all disappear, she'll at least go find this and read it. She may not want to hear now, but she will then."

"That's a great idea." Jordan grabbed a bagel off the plate in the middle of the table. Kat had decided since they had to get such an early start to the airport that she might as well have a portable breakfast ready. "I might need to do that too. I don't know how long I'll be in Texas, but if I'm still there when semester starts again, I think reaching college kids will be even harder than these women coming into the pregnancy center."

Kat thought about the stories she saw on the news and social media. It appeared that many high school and college-aged students cared more about defending abortion and using the correct pronoun than they did about following God's moral code, but surely there were still some. Some who believed in the right and wrong detailed in the Bible, who feared Hell and wanted to live a life pleasing to God. "You might be right, but I'm sure there are some amazing younger people like yourself. You attended a church back there, didn't you?"

Jordan brushed a strand of her blonde hair behind her ear. "Yeah, a lot of good people went to my church, but there were others, even at church, who definitely did not agree with my view of Jesus. They called me a bigot, a hater, and basically told me that Jesus loves everyone, so even if what I'm saying is true that He'll let everyone into Heaven."

Kat reached out to touch Jordan's arm. "I'm sorry. It's hard everywhere, but I can see why the younger generation would be so much harder. We've definitely confused them the last few years. Even most churches are no longer teaching the hard messages for fear of losing their members."

Jordan nodded. "I mean, I know the Bible says it will

be harder for Christians in the final days, but I don't think I knew it would be this hard. Did you see on the news that a local pharmacy just got sued for not carrying the Morning After pill? There's a dozen pharmacies within spitting distance of that one that chooses not to carry abortion pills, but because someone was inconvenienced, they feel it's okay to sue them."

"Yeah, I heard." Stories like these were becoming the norm instead of the outliers. Kat watched the news only because she felt it was important to know what was going on around them, to watch for any signs that Jesus might be coming back soon. If she weren't doing this job, she would definitely avoid it. The news was never happy. It was always filled with murder or, as Jordan stated, cases of Christian organizations being sued for their beliefs. "I'm afraid it will get even worse once we're gone. I just hope I can reach Raven in time."

A silence fell between them for a moment before Jordan cleared her throat. "Speaking of time, we should probably be heading out if we want to reach the airport in time."

Kat sighed and shut her computer screen. "Yes, I suppose we should. I'm going to miss you, Jordan."

Jordan's bottom lip folded under as her eyes grew misty. "I'm going to miss you too, but we can keep in touch." She held up her cell phone and wiggled it. "At least we have these."

"That we do." The irony of it was not lost on Kat. Technology was separating people from God, stealing their time and attention. It was separating people from each other, but it was also a way to stay connected, a way she would be able to check in with Jordan, and they could still share about their days. Odd how it could serve both purposes. "Okay, do you have everything?"

Jordan glanced down at her suitcase. "Yep, I traveled light. Maybe now I know why."

Kat marveled at Jordan's demeanor as she led the way out to the car. Here was a girl so much younger than herself, who'd had terrible things happen to her, who was still a baby Christian, yet she seemed to possess a willing spirit to go anywhere and do anything. If only more people could be like that.

The drive to the airport was quiet as if they were both unsure of what to say or if anything needed to be said, but as soon as Kat pulled up to the curb, the hesitation broke.

"Call me as soon as you land and let me know you're safe, okay?"

Jordan nodded, her eyes glistening with unshed tears. "I will. Tell Patrick and Maddie goodbye for me too?"

"Of course." As Kat hugged Jordan one last time, she felt in her bones that it was the last time she would see the girl on Earth, and a part of her didn't want to let go. In the short time she had known her, Jordan had become like family and letting her leave almost felt like losing Stella all over again. Still, she knew it was something Jordan had to do. Kat just wished it didn't feel so hard to let go.

Jordan wiped a tiny tear from the corner of her eye as she walked to her gate. Going home felt right, but she would miss Kat and Patrick and Maddie. They might not be her blood family, but she'd felt closer to them in the few weeks she had known them than she had to her own mother in the last few years. She would definitely miss her tea talks with Kat.

The crowd at her gate was sparse, and she scanned the vicinity for any sign of Jeremy. He'd said he was on the same flight, yet she hadn't seen him yet.

"Is this seat taken?"

The deep timbre of his voice sent a shiver down her spine, and she looked up to find his caring eyes staring intently at her. "Where did you come from?" She had been scanning the area as she approached, and she couldn't understand how she might have missed him.

His eyes twinkled as his lips pulled into a sly smile. "I have my ways." He set a tan backpack down and plopped into the chair next to her. "So, do you want to tell me why you're heading back to Texas?"

Jordan took a deep breath as she searched his eyes. Could she trust him? The coincidences behind their meetings were strange, but something deep inside told her she could. "I'm going back to see my son."

A look of something akin to surprise flashed in his eyes, but he didn't seem completely shocked. "You have a son." Even the way he said it sounded more like a statement than a question.

"I do, but I gave him up for adoption. I was too young and…" She let her voice trail off. He didn't need to know about her rape. It would be bad enough if he thought she was promiscuous, but too many people looked at her differently after she told them she'd been raped. She didn't want Jeremy to as well. "Anyway, I felt the need to see him one last time."

"One last time?" Jeremy's voice held a teasing note. "Are you planning on dying soon?"

She knew he was kidding, probably trying to make light of the heavy situation she had just laid at his feet, but it just reminded her of her mission. She was supposed to be telling people about Jesus, saving as many souls as she could before the rapture, but she hadn't talked with anyone since she lost her visions. Could she tell Jeremy? She had no idea if he was a believer or what it might take to convince him, but she could try. If seeing her son didn't bring her gift back, this would be her new normal anyway.

"Do you believe in God, Jeremy?

10

FRIDAY AFTERNOON

"Well, you're here early. Becoming a regular gym rat, aren't you?"

Kat smiled at Brian. While she didn't mind becoming a gym rat, she was really here early because she couldn't stand sitting at home alone any longer. The suspension was killing her as was the waiting game her supervisor was playing with her. The board was still discussing, he'd said in his latest email, but Kat was pretty sure he knew the outcome and was simply stringing her along a little longer because he could.

"Yeah, well, that's what happens when you have a lot of time on your hands."

He tilted his head at her. "Time? Are you a teacher off for the summer?"

Kat chuckled. "No, I'm an oncologist, but I'm-" She

stopped herself. Somehow, she felt that sharing why she had so much time would set Brian back instead of pushing him closer to God. The light still hadn't left him entirely. "I'm in between cases," she finished, hoping he wouldn't call her on the fib.

"Well, it's good to have down time," he said. "I could use some of that myself."

"Indeed." Kat flashed a small smile and then nodded toward the locker room. "Guess I'll go get changed."

Brian flashed her a wave and then reached for the phone which had just begun to ring.

Kat continued her trek around the bags, but she was stopped again before she made it to the locker room.

"Kat? You have a minute?"

She backed up and poked her head into the weight room. Jason stood facing her, his weight shifting from one foot to the other. "Sure, Jason, what's up?"

"I wanted to thank you for what you said the other day."

"Of course. You're welcome." She smiled at him and turned to leave but his hand caught her arm and stilled her. Slowly, she turned back to face him, both excited and scared of what he was about to say.

"No one has believed in me in a long time. In fact, I'm not even sure I've believed in myself lately, but your words hit me." He paused and Kat could see his Adam's apple bob in his throat. "Anyway, I wanted to see if you might like to have lunch with me tomorrow."

His insecurity swam in his eyes, and Kat wanted to say yes, not only for him but for herself as well. She knew her time on Earth was limited, but Jason was someone she was supposed to reach anyway, and she was losing her mind sitting at home. However, would she push him farther from God if she said yes, but then decided it wouldn't work? Or worse, if the rapture happened and she disappeared on him?

Kat bit her lip as she thought of how to answer. There were pros and cons to both answers. It was just lunch, and she could use the time to share with him. "Okay, lunch." They were just two words, but Kat felt like a lot hinged on those two words. She just wasn't sure if it was a lot of good or a lot of bad.

Raven scanned the gym for Kat as she stepped through the front glass door. She'd seen the girl's Mini Cooper outside, and she was determined to get some answers. Kat was either a liar or a witch, and Raven was going to find out which.

Brian flashed her a wave as she passed his desk, but she was too focused on her mission to respond. A few other guys were in the gym early, hitting bags or running on the treadmill, but besides them, the gym was quiet. This was normally her favorite time to come, not only because it was before the place filled with noise and the smell of sweat, but also because it was the best time to catch Jason alone.

Jason. Interesting that she didn't see him. Normally by this time, he would be wiping down the bags or vacuuming the floor, but he was nowhere in sight. Had he taken a day off? She knew he did that occasionally, normally when he drank too much the night before and was suffering from a hangover, but he'd seemed in high spirits yesterday.

She poked her head into the weight room as she passed. Jason was at the bench press again focused on the bar he held in his hands. Raven wanted to stay and watch his muscles flex, but he was not her primary goal right now. She needed to find Kat.

Raven continued to the locker room and there she found Kat pulling gym clothes out of her bag. "We need to talk."

Kat looked up, surprise covering her face. "Okay, about what?" There was hesitation in her voice, but she set down her clothes and waited for Raven to continue.

"About what you said. About my future."

Kat's eyes shifted to the doorway. "Are you sure you want to have this conversation here? What I have to tell you is going to sound a little crazy."

"Here is as good a place as any. I'm not going anywhere with you until I know what's going on."

Kat sighed and patted the bench next to her. "You better sit down then."

Though Raven was hesitant to get too close to Kat in case she was a witch, she sat down on the bench and waited for the girl to begin.

Kat tapped her lip for a moment as if debating how to begin. Then she took a deep breath and opened her mouth. "I told you the other day that I began coming in after my friend died. I was angry and I didn't know how to channel that anger, but I also thought I was going crazy."

Though she didn't want to, Raven could empathize with Kat. She hadn't lost a best friend - she wasn't sure she'd ever really had one - but she remembered feeling like she was going crazy when her world turned upside down at the tender age of twelve.

"I started seeing lights around people. Not everyone but enough that I couldn't dismiss it as hallucinations."

A vise began to squeeze on Raven's lungs. Kat saw things too?

Kat paused and licked her lips. "I didn't know what the lights were, so I tried to ignore them, but then I began having dreams of my best friend telling me that I needed to listen. I didn't know what she meant, but then a girl from Texas showed up and told me God had sent her to help me understand my gift."

Crazy wasn't the word Raven would have chosen for the words coming out of Kat's mouth. Crazy would barely scratch the surface, but she forced her jaw shut to let Kat continue.

"Jordan, that was the girl, arriving really shook me up, and I confided in my mother who then told me that I used to see Jesus and talk to him when I was little."

A small snort escaped Raven's lips, and she shook her head. This was too much. "I'm sorry. You saw Jesus? I don't believe in Jesus." Kat was either battier than an old cat lady or on drugs. Raven just wasn't sure which.

"I know." Kat stared at her with an intensity that immediately dried up Raven's scoffing. "I wasn't sure I believed my mother either; I certainly had no memory of seeing Jesus, but then an angel appeared to me and it grew pretty hard to deny."

Drugs were definitely taking the lead. Raven didn't think crazy cat ladies even went this far off the reservation. "An angel? Appeared to you? Did she float down on a cloud and play a harp? Or did she look like Roma Downey?" Raven couldn't believe she was giving any time to this nonsense.

"No, *he* didn't." Kat seemed unfazed by Raven's ridicule which unnerved her.

"He came into my office and unfurled his wings, glowing brighter than anything I'd ever seen. He told me the lights I see are people who are being protected by angels while they decide to follow Jesus or not."

"Really? So you just see angels sitting on people's shoulders? Do you see the devils too?" Condescension dripped from Raven's voice. This was worse than some hokey after school special, and she was determined to get a rise out of Kat. Her calm demeanor was unnatural.

"No, I don't see devils, but I think you might see demons." Kat's serious tone wiped the smile from Raven's face.

"What do you mean?" Images of the dark shapes she'd been seeing the last few days assaulted her mind, and she shook her head to clear them. "I don't believe in demons, so how could I see them?"

"I know you saw something the other day, Raven. Something that scared you. Now, I was afraid when I first saw the lights, but I was scared because I thought I was going crazy, not because the lights themselves frightened me."

Raven's defensive shields kicked into place. "You don't know what you're talking about."

"I know the angel, Micah, said I had to find you. I don't know why, but he said you were important in the next phase."

Micah? Had she just said Micah? Could it be the same mysterious Micah Raven had met? No, that would be impossible. There was no way she had spoken with an angel. Besides Micah was a common name. She decided to let it go and focus on the last comment. "What next phase?"

Kat rubbed the back of her neck and let out a long, slow breath. "I don't know for sure. He didn't tell me, but what he did say was that the rapture was going to come soon, and you would be important after we were gone."

Raven's brow lifted. "Gone? What do you mean gone?"

"When the rapture happens, Raven, all believers in Christ will disappear. At least that's the accepted theory. Some believe we may leave behind clothes or disappear completely. Either way, I believe we will be gone and half the population will be left wondering what happened to us. After that, the tribulation begins, and it isn't pretty according to the Bible."

Raven's dream flashed into her mind. The child disappearing in her hands. All the kids in the gym being gone. The driver who said no one was in the car coming at him. Could all this be true? Her head spun as she tried to make sense of it. She didn't believe in God, didn't believe in angels or demons. She believed in monsters. There'd been enough of those in her life, but they were human monsters - nothing supernatural.

"I know it's a lot to take in. It was for me too, but I'm supposed to help you, Raven."

The pleading in Kat's voice interrupted her inner

turmoil, and she stared into her eyes. "What if I don't want your help?"

Kat sighed as she changed back into street clothes after her workout. She'd thought there'd been a moment when she had been reaching Raven, when maybe the girl was opening up and listening, but then she'd shut down again.

"What if I don't want your help?" Kat hadn't known what to say when Raven had posed that question. Of course, she couldn't make Raven do anything. All she could do was give her the information and be there to answer any questions she might have, but Micah had said this was her job, and since she was still on suspension it was the only job she seemed to have at the moment. She felt like she was failing miserably.

Raven hadn't spoken to her after that - hadn't even looked at her, but Kat could feel the negative energy radiating her direction from the girl. She didn't know what it was going to take to reach her.

Hoisting her bag on her shoulder, she exited the locker room, waving to Jason as she left. He still had the light on his shoulder too, but she'd received no more words to say to him either. Perhaps she would at lunch tomorrow. Lunch. The thought sent her insides twisting. She still didn't know if accepting lunch with him had been a good idea. What she did know was that she had to be disappointing Micah.

Kat slid into her seat and rested her head on the steering wheel for a moment. What was she going to do? "I need help," she whispered. With Jordan gone and the suspension over her head, her job felt more impossible than ever.

"Have faith."

The words were not so much audible as felt in her bones, and while they would normally give comfort, today they felt empty. She wanted to have faith, but nothing she was doing seemed to be making a difference. Kat picked up her cell and dialed Patrick.

"Hey, you okay if I bring dinner and eat with you guys? I don't want to be alone this evening." She bit the inside of her lip as she waited for his response. Though she doubted he would say no, the thought of the possibility of spending the evening in her empty apartment churned her stomach even more than her upcoming lunch date.

The smile was evident in his voice when he answered. "Sounds good. Maddie would love to see you."

Kat smiled as she started the car. Everything else might be going sideways, but at least she had Patrick and Maddie.

"So, you're telling me that you get visions of people's sins?"

Jordan cringed at the tone of Jeremy's voice. "I know it sounds crazy, but it isn't always sins. Sometimes, I get words I'm supposed to say to people to help them feel better."

Jeremy smiled and placed a hand on her arm. Immediately, heat spread throughout her body from his touch. "I don't think you're crazy."

She looked up at him. How could he not think she was crazy when she sometimes thought she was? "You don't?"

His smile widened, and light shone from his eyes. "Jordan, do you not find our meetings to be fortuitous?"

"I..." She paused. She had been thinking that very thing when she got his text message. The odds of them meeting once were high, but the odds of them returning to Texas on the same flight were pretty astronomical. "What are you saying?"

"I'm saying that our meetings have not been by accident. They have been planned."

"Planned? But how?" Jordan should be terrified at this point. His words sounded an awful lot like a stalker's words, but she didn't feel afraid. Only curious.

The light seemed to radiate from every inch of his face. "Because I'm an angel, Jordan. Your angel."

"Final call for United flight 762." Jordan barely heard the announcement as she stared at Jeremy. An angel? On one hand it made perfect sense, but on the other... he didn't look like an angel.

"Come on, that was our call." He stood and pulled her to her feet beside him. "We better get on the plane before we miss our flight. I can see you have a lot of questions, but we'll have plenty of time to talk."

Talk? How was she supposed to talk to him after that bombshell? She let him lead her to the boarding door, but she had no idea what she was supposed to say to him now.

11

FRIDAY EVENING

"So, how are you dealing with everything?" Patrick asked as Kat helped him clear the dishes after dinner.

Kat chuckled slightly as she rinsed a cup in the sink. "I feel like I should be asking you that question. You're the one having to adjust to being a single father."

"True, and that's difficult, but I'm not the one seeing angels and trying to convince people to believe her."

Kat turned off the water and sighed. "I spoke with Raven today. She listened, but I don't know if she really heard me. If she wanted to hear me. I feel like I'm going crazy, Patrick. This isn't how I saw my life going at all."

He set down the towel he had been using to wipe the table and crossed to her. His hands grabbed her arms, and he stared into her eyes. "Life doesn't always turn out the way we planned it, but you have an amazing mission, and you are not crazy." He chuckled and let go of her arms. "Stella used to tell me how strong you were, and how she wished she could be as strong."

Kat bit the inside of her lip. "I don't feel very strong right now."

Maddie chose that moment to burst into the kitchen. "Aunt Kat, will you play Frozen with me?"

Kat smiled at the young girl. How she wished she could go back to that age, to being so carefree and simple. Even though the girl had lost her mother, she didn't let it consume her. "Sure, honey."

"Have faith, Kat," Patrick said as she left the room. "Everything will work out. You'll see."

"Yeah, Aunt Kat, have faith," Maddie said as she pulled Kat to her room. "Mommy said I would get to see her again soon."

Kat planted her feet and stared down at Maddie. "Mommy? When did you talk to your mom, Maddie?"

Maddie shrugged. "In my dream last night. She found me at the park and gave me a hug. Then she told me it wouldn't be much longer until we were together again. I'm glad. I miss my mommy."

A tiny seed of jealousy sprouted in Kat's stomach, but she wasn't sure if she was jealous because Stella was now visiting Maddie's dreams instead of her own, or if she was jealous of Maddie's simple faith and acceptance.

"You're a pretty amazing kid, you know that, right, Monkey?"

"You're amazing too, Aunt Kat. Now, do you want to be Elsa or Anna?"

An angel. The words collided together in Jordan's head as she stowed her suitcase and then sat down. So, that's why she had been so comfortable around him. It made sense, but her mind was still reeling. Jeremy had just dropped a bombshell on her, and she wasn't sure she was entirely caught up yet.

"Why do I need an angel?" Jordan asked as Jeremy plopped down beside her. Her brain felt like it was pulsing out of her head.

Kindness shone from his face as he smiled patiently at her and opened his mouth to explain. "You can't see them, Jordan, but there are demons all around. They are waiting for us to slip, to take our eyes off you so they can sow their seeds. They know that you are important, and they want to take you out of commission. Fortunately, they haven't been able to reach you, but it's why they've gone after your son."

Jordan's head shot up. "That baby I've been seeing. He's my son?"

Jeremy nodded. "He is, and he is in danger. We stopped your visions so you would know that you had to go and help him."

Jordan swallowed as fear constricted her heart. "And that shape that I've seen leaning over him? That's a demon?"

He nodded again. "For now, they are simply watching him, but they will strike soon. We have to protect him."

"Why? I mean, don't get me wrong, I want him protected, but if all believers are going to be raptured soon, doesn't that include children?"

Jeremy's eyes shifted from her gaze, and the vein in his neck bulged.

"What? What aren't you telling me? Surely, you're not saying that babies and children get left behind?"

"No, they will be taken."

"Then what?"

He returned his gaze to her. "Losing your son would have a profound impact on you. Enough to skew your visions and influence those around you negatively."

"So, you're saying if my son dies, then I start leading people astray?"

"We won't let that happen." Jeremy touched her arm, but even the warmth of his touch didn't dispel the coldness that had sprouted in Jordan's stomach from his words.

Raven dropped her gym bag on the floor and headed for the shower. Angels? Demons? Rapture? Tribulation? Kat was even crazier than she thought. The girl seriously had a screw loose.... But what if she was right? What if there was something supernatural going on here? Raven had no other explanations for the dreams or the black shapes. Plus, there was the mysterious Micah. She'd dismissed the idea originally that he was Kat's angel, but what if he was?

She could find out. After her shower, she could return to work and check out the room again. If it was still an office, she could do some snooping to find out about Micah, and if it wasn't... well, then she might have to consider Kat's story a little more closely.

Raven turned on the hot water and peeled off her clothes. She stepped into the pelting water, letting it soothe her muscles. Workouts always left her tense, but dealing with this, whatever it was, was making it worse. Her hand massaged the spot on her back near her shoulder blade that always seemed to carry the worst of it as her mind wandered.

If Kat's story was true, why would she be important? She was no one, an abused teen who'd turned into a hardened woman. She cared for no one, and she certainly didn't treat her body like a temple. Why on earth would she matter if the tribulation did happen?

Then suddenly the room grew bright. Raven placed one hand on the wall of the shower and the other over her eyes. What was happening to her?

"Do you know why we named you Raven, honey?"

The dark haired girl stared up at her father from the swing. "No. Why, daddy?"

"Because you are special. Your mother and I waited a long time to have you. In fact, we had given up hope that we would ever have children, and then your mother had a dream. She dreamt that an angel told her you would be born and that you would be a guide for people when the time came. Ravens don't mind the darkness, but they can guide people to the light. I think one day you'll be an important guide, Raven."

The little girl's laugh sounded like tinkling bells. "Daddy, you're so silly. I'm too little to guide people."

The image faded and Raven gasped. Was that a memory? She had so few of her father it was hard to be sure. He'd been killed shortly after her ninth birthday, mugged in the parking lot as he placed Christmas gifts into his car. There'd been no Christmas that year, and Raven's life had changed after that. Her mother had turned first to alcohol and then to men in an attempt to fill the void in her life. Raven had retreated into the darkness, dressing in black and letting negativity fill her soul.

What had her father said? That she was a guide? She was supposed to lead people to the light? What light? Kat was the one who saw lights; Jordan only saw dark shapes. Could he have meant the light after the rapture? Was she supposed to guide people after all the Christians were gone? Though she wanted it not to be true, the answer felt right in her soul. Yes, she really needed to find Micah again.

Half an hour later, she turned off the Jeep and stared at the building. The sun hadn't quite set yet, and there were still a few cars in the parking lot. Could one of them be Micah's? Did he even drive? Only one way to find out.

She flashed her badge as she passed the reception desk on her way to the elevator. A part of her feared the woman would ask her where she was going, but the woman seemed not to care. Raven punched the button and stepped inside when the doors opened.

A moment later, the ding of the elevator broke the silence, and Raven stepped out, letting the doors close behind her. The floor appeared empty, but Raven forced her feet to head in the direction of room 144.

When she reached the door, she knocked, but no voice beckoned her inside this time. She placed her hand on the door knob and turned, expecting to find it locked, but it swung open to an empty room.

Raven flicked on the light and stared in disbelief. The office had been minimal when she had visited with Micah before, but there was nothing here now. No desk, no phone, not even any indentations on the carpet where the furniture had been. It was like nothing had been in this office for a very long time. So what exactly had she seen and who had she spoken with?

"So, are we just going to knock and ask to see the baby?" Jordan stared out the window of the rental car at the cream-colored rambler with a dark brown trim. After landing the night before, Jeremy had rented them a car while Jordan had rented a hotel room. She had turned in early, her mind still processing the fact that he was an angel. She had no idea how he had spent the night because he'd told her angels didn't need to sleep, but she'd been too overwhelmed to ask him anything more.

His eyes scanned the area. "I'm afraid we are going to have to take the baby and the parents and run."

Jordan blinked at him. "We're going to kidnap them? What if they won't go with us?"

"Then we will do what we must. It is important that we get the baby out alive."

Jordan's eyes narrowed. Why did she feel as if Jeremy wasn't telling her the whole story? "How many demons are there, Jeremy?"

"At the house currently? I sense only one which is why we must move now."

"No, not just at the house. In the world. How many are around us every day?"

His stare chilled her to the bone. "More than you could count, Jordan, but we can have that discussion another day."

"So, why is he so important? There have to be many other people at risk." She didn't know why she was asking or why his answer was so important to her. Why couldn't she just accept his help and save her son?

Jeremy sighed, and though his gaze continued to flick back to the house, he humored her. "There are many important people at risk, but there are others reaching out to them, watching over them. You are my responsibility as is your son, so can we please go now?"

There was more going on than Jeremy was telling her; Jordan was sure of it, but now was not the time to argue. She opened her door, took a deep breath, and walked toward the front door.

The doorbell made a soft chime as Jordan pushed the lighted button. A moment later, the door swung open and Heather Blakely smiled at her. Fresh-faced and blonde, her hair was pulled back in a ponytail, and she exuded comfort in her loose fitting cut-off jeans and t-shirt.

A look of surprise flitted across her blue eyes before a smile turned up the corners of her mouth. "Jordan? What are you doing here?"

Jordan took a deep breath and forced what she hoped was a smile in return. "Hi, Heather. Are you busy?"

Heather's eyes narrowed as she looked Jordan over more closely. No doubt, she was curious as to why Jordan was on her doorstep unannounced. There might even be a piece of her that wondered if Jordan would try to reclaim her son, though the adoption paperwork made that impossible. "Not at the moment, but Samuel will be waking up from his nap soon."

Samuel. She hadn't known what the Blakelys had named him - hadn't wanted to know. It had been hard enough holding him at the hospital and looking down into his clear blue eyes - eyes that had never seen evil and knew her only as the one who had given him life for ten months. Somehow, Samuel seemed to fit him. It wasn't what Jordan might have named him had she kept him, but it felt right in her head.

"I was hoping I could talk to you for a bit and maybe see Samuel when he wakes up?" Jordan looked to Jeremy for help, but he was no longer by her side. Where had he gone? She swallowed and prayed that Heather wouldn't send her packing.

"Of course you can come in." Heather stepped back and held the door for Jordan to enter, but a look of caution still danced across her defined features. "What's this about though, Jordan? I thought you didn't want to be in his life right now."

"I-" Jordan opened her mouth to answer, but before she could, Samuel's cry pierced the air followed quickly by a shout from Jeremy.

"Jordan, get the baby and run!"

Jordan glanced at Heather to gauge her reaction, but Heather hadn't seemed to hear Jeremy. Instead, she had sauntered over to a table where a baby monitor sat and was staring at the screen. "That's odd. He usually sleeps longer."

"Heather, we have to go. Grab whatever you need for Samuel. Is Dave here?"

The expression on Heather's face morphed from caution to fear. "No, he's at work. What do you mean go? Go where?"

The sound of metal clanging against metal reached Jordan's ears, along with some high pitched noise that she couldn't place but sent the hairs on her arm standing at attention like they had whenever someone had run their nails down a chalkboard.

"Jordan, hurry." Jeremy's voice sounded strained and a loud crash punctuated it.

"What was that?" Heather's head whipped toward the hallway behind her. "Was that from Samuel's room?"

"Yes, Samuel is in danger. Please, grab anything you need for him. I'll grab him and meet you outside. Go!" Jordan's voice took on an authority she didn't feel, but it spurred Heather into action.

As she hurried to gather items for Samuel, Jordan walked toward the noise. Samuel's cries were louder as she approached, and a bright light shone underneath the crack of his door.

Unsure exactly what to expect, Jordan flung the door open and froze momentarily. Jeremy no longer looked like the boy she had met. Golden wings spread from his back and in his hand he held a sword. His chiseled face had a hardened fierceness she had never seen before. She could tell he was fighting someone or something, but she could not see it - only Jeremy.

He glanced her direction as he parried and thrust his sword. "Grab him and run." The loud voice seemed to fill the room and permeate every inch of her body. A shrill screech filled the air at his words, and a chill raced down Jordan's back.

She hesitated only a second before rushing forward and scooping Samuel up in her arms. His cries were drowned by the screeching and she squeezed him to her chest. She snatched his bear and blanket up and then raced from the room.

Heather stood at the front door, fear in her wide eyes, and a diaper bag slung over her shoulder. "What's going on, Jordan?"

"I'll tell you in the car. Come on."

Jordan hit the key fob before they reached the vehicle and motioned for Heather to get in the passenger seat. Then she handed over her son, staring just a moment at his beautiful face, before racing around to her side of the car and firing up the engine. She didn't like leaving Jeremy, but surely he would get in touch with her when it was safe to come back and get him.

Heather squeezed Samuel to her chest, and her voice was still laced with fear when she spoke again. "Jordan, what is going on?"

"I'll tell you everything when we get some place safe. Can we go to Dave's work?"

Heather nodded and issued directions as Jordan drove.

Kat took a deep breath as she pulled open the door of the restaurant. Jason had picked a small, quaint venue for which she was glad.

He sat at a table in the back and waved her over when their eyes connected. He really was quite handsome, albeit in an unconventional way. Having lost his hair years ago, he kept it shaved and shiny on top, but it worked for him.

His dark beard and mustache were neatly groomed and kept his face from looking too thin, but his best feature was his smile by far. Though his bottom teeth were crooked, his smile held an authenticity that was hard to find.

"Thanks for coming. I wasn't sure you'd actually show up."

She smiled down at him as she pulled out a chair. "I wasn't sure I was going to either." A look of hurt flashed across his hazel eyes, and Kat quickly continued, "But not because of you."

"Because of your friend?" he asked.

"Partly." How much should she tell him? She wanted to help him but not send him running.

"Well, I'm glad you came."

It seemed like a good place to end the conversation, so Kat let it rest. There would be plenty of time to bring it up later.

After the waitress dropped off menus and they both ordered, Kat focused on Jason again. "So, how long have you been working at the gym?"

Jason lifted his water glass and took a sip. "About three years, but I trained with Brian when I was younger."

"How much younger?" She wasn't exactly sure of Jason's age, but she pegged him to be about her age - mid thirties.

"Since I was seventeen. I've been fighting a long time,

and then I joined the military for a few years. Then I got married and divorced and ended up back here."

"Wow, that sounds like a lot." Kat ran a finger down her water glass. "So marriage didn't work for you?"

Jason chuffed and offered a crooked smile. "I'm kind of a hot mess and so was she. Two hot messes don't mix well together unfortunately."

"Why do you think you're a hot mess? I know I don't know you well, but you seem pretty grounded to me."

He took another drink and then smiled again, but it was sadder this time. "I put on a good show, but at thirty-four, this wasn't where I saw my life."

Kat understood that thought. Though she technically had the job she'd worked for, she was suspended at the moment which had certainly not been in her plan. Plus, she didn't have the husband and kids she thought she would by now. "It's not too late to change it, you know?"

"I don't know. You have to want more and while I do, I don't feel like working harder to get it right now."

Kat's heart hurt at how broken he sounded - him and Raven both - and she wondered what his story was. What her story was. And then she wondered if the rest of the people she saw lights around were just as broken.

"Anyway, that isn't why I asked you to lunch. I wanted to know more about you because you seem so different."

And that was her cue. "I'm not that different from you,

Jason. I have the job I've always wanted though I'm on suspension at the moment."

His brow lifted in a silent question, and she chuckled. "I'll tell you more about that in a minute. I thought my life was in order until Stella died. Then I had this crazy anger that took ahold of me. It wasn't until I found my way back to God that I found peace."

Jason leaned back in his chair. "God, huh? I'm not sure I believe in God."

"How can you look around at the world and not see that someone amazing, someone much larger than us created it?"

"Oh, I believe a higher power created the world, but I'm not sure whatever it was stuck around. There's too much suffering in the world for them to still be here. Plus, all these different religions believe their god is the right god. Who can really say for sure theirs is the only way?"

Kat sighed. Jason needed more help than she'd initially thought, and he was the hardest type of person to reach. He wasn't an atheist because he believed in a higher power, but he didn't seem to care or realize how much he needed God. She feared he would need to see a miracle before he put his faith in God, and she could only hope he would live long enough to do that.

"I can certainly understand your skepticism. It's hard to believe in something you can't see, and I was right there after Stella died."

"So what changed it for you? What brought you back to God?"

She didn't sense hostility in his answer, only curiosity, so she decided to take a chance. "Honestly? Because I saw an angel."

He leaned forward again. "An angel?"

Kat nodded. "Yep. After Stella died, I began seeing lights around people. Then this angel appeared in my office and told me those lights were angels protecting people who were thinking about giving their life to God. He told me I was supposed to talk to them. To you."

His eyebrow arched. "To me? You're saying I have a light?"

"You do. The day I told you that you mattered, it was because God told me to."

"But I don't believe in God, so why would I have a light?"

"I don't know, but I know that God loves you even when you claim to not believe in Him. I'm not exactly sure how the rest of it all works. I just know the angel told me to talk to people and especially Raven."

"Raven? I don't think she's much of a believer either."

"No, she isn't, but that doesn't change my job."

The waitress arrived then and placed the food down, ending the conversation for the time being. Kat hoped she would have another chance, but at least she had gotten to plant another seed.

Raven smoothed her skirt as she stepped out of the car. She wasn't concerned with impressing Jason tonight, but looking good never hurt when it came to getting what you wanted.

The hum of conversation spilled out of the bar as Raven pulled the door open, and she blinked to adjust to the dimmer lighting. Her eyes scanned the area as she made her way to the bar where Jason was working. Most of the patrons appeared to be couples or tight knit groups. Not too surprising as this bar was casual enough to be a decent hangout spot on weekends.

"Hey, Raven, tequila again?" Jason asked as she reached the mahogany bar.

"Sure, but I also have a question for you." She smiled and batted her eyes.

He lifted one eyebrow in a silent question before grabbing the tequila from the shelf behind him and filling a shot glass rimmed with salt. "Shoot."

"Do you happen to have Kat's number?"

The other eyebrow lifted as well. "Kat? The girl from the gym that you hate?" He placed a slice of lime on the glass and set it in front of her. "Why do you want Kat's number?"

Raven poured the shot contents down her throat

before answering. She didn't even bother with the lime or the salt. "I need to ask her something. She said she knew something about my future, and I dismissed her at first. However, recent events have caused me to reconsider."

"Recent events, huh?" He folded his arms across his chest and leaned back against the back counter. "Would this have to do with the dark shapes?"

Raven smiled though his avoidance of her question was starting to annoy her. She wished she hadn't told him about the shapes. "I'll tell you everything soon. After I talk to Kat. Maybe we can pull an all-nighter and I'll fill you in." She wiggled her eyebrows suggestively. "But first I need to know what it all means. Now, I know you've been chatting with her during class, so do you happen to have her number?"

He considered her a moment before reaching into his back pocket and pulling out his wallet. "I do actually. In fact, I had lunch with her today. It seems she needs to talk to you too."

Anger sparked within Raven, and her jaw clenched. Kat had gone to lunch with Jason even after she'd said she wasn't interested and she'd talked about Raven? It appeared she had more than a few questions for Kat. "Lunch, huh?"

Jason smiled and shook his head at her as if she were being ridiculous. "Yes, lunch, but relax. She's way too religious for me. So, if I give you this, do you promise me it's only to ask questions and not to harass her?"

Raven took a deep breath to keep her irritation from snapping at him. If there was nothing going on between them, then why was he being so protective of Kat? "Yes, I promise. I only want to talk to her." After I give her a piece of my mind, Raven thought to herself, but Jason didn't need to know that.

He held her gaze a moment longer, searching her eyes for deception, before opening his wallet and pulling out a small piece of paper. "This is her cell number. She told me to call if I had any questions or needed to talk."

Raven removed her phone and snapped a picture of the number. "Thanks, Jason, I appreciate it." She smiled and placed a five dollar bill on the bar to cover her drink before heading toward the exit to make the call in a quieter environment.

Her fingers shook slightly as she dialed the number. Did she really want to do this? It felt like opening Pandora's Box, and somehow she knew it was going to change things forever.

"This is Kat."

No turning back now. "Kat, it's Raven. We need to talk."

Kat had no idea what to expect when the doorbell rang, but she was not prepared for the slap that landed across her cheek. Her hand flew to the angry red mark. "What was that for?"

"That was for going to lunch with Jason. I told you he was mine."

"You came all the way over here to slap me?" Kat couldn't believe the nerve of Raven.

"No, I do have questions for you, but I couldn't ask them until we had this sorted out. Now, are you going to let me in?"

Kat chuckled at the irony. The Bible said to turn the other cheek, but she hadn't thought she would ever really have to do that to reach someone. Evidently Raven believed in being the exception to the rules.

"Sure, come on in. My lunch with Jason wasn't really a date just so you know," Kat said as she shut the door behind them.

"I know. He told me you were too religious for him."

The condescension in Raven's voice was thick, but Kat let it slide. She had known halfway through the lunch that she and Jason would never work out even if the rapture wasn't imminent.

"Would you like some tea?" Kat asked as Raven sat on her couch. She'd never seen the girl look nervous, and she certainly wouldn't have expected it after the angry greeting, but it filled the air around her now like an invisible field.

"Um, no thanks." Raven's eyes scanned the room and though she knew she shouldn't care, Kat wondered what she thought. Her living room was decorated minimally. Kat wasn't a fan of clutter, but she did love books and photography, and they were dispersed throughout the room.

"So-" Kat wasn't sure where to go from here. Did she ask Raven why she was here? What had changed her mind? Or did she wait for Raven to speak first?

"So, you're probably wondering why I called you." Raven's eyes focused on Kat.

"I must confess that I am. You certainly didn't seem open to what I was saying before." Kat lowered herself into the chair closest to Raven.

"Yeah, I wasn't. I'm still not sure I am, but I've had some things happen that I can't explain, and I guess I'm hoping you can help."

Kat nodded, wishing Raven had accepted the offer for tea. She could really use something in her hands right now. "I'll do what I can. Do you want to tell me what happened?"

Raven bit her lip and ran her hands down her skirt - one that was too short for Kat's taste - before speaking. "First, can you tell me what your angel looked like? Micah, right?"

Micah? Kat certainly hadn't been expecting that question. "Yeah. His name is Micah. Well, before I knew he was an angel, he was pretty regular looking. Dark hair, blue eyes, chiseled features - almost like they were etched out of stone which makes a lot more sense now. Why?"

"Would it be possible for him to make something out of nothing or make me think I saw something that wasn't really there?" Raven's eyes slid to the side as she finished the question. Something had definitely rattled her.

"Yeah, I think it might. When I was struggling with my anger, I decided to see a therapist. I went to this building and sat on this woman's couch in an office, but when I went back a few days later, the building was boarded up. No one had been there for years. Micah told me later that the therapist I had spoken with had really been an angel. Is that what you mean?"

Raven's eyes widened. "Yeah, that's exactly what I mean. I went to work early one day because the dreams were keeping me up-"

Kat leaned forward, interrupting Raven. "Wait, dreams?"

"I'll get to them in a minute. Anyway, I went in early and I got this call on my cell that I needed to come to this office upstairs. I'd never been there before, but there was a man with dark hair and blue eyes who introduced himself as Micah. He said he was my counselor and he wanted me to talk about the shapes I was seeing and my-" Her mouth snapped shut.

Kat wanted to urge her to continue, but it was clear Raven wasn't comfortable discussing whatever else he had asked her about.

Raven ran a hand through her hair before continuing. "Anyway, last night, I decided to return to ask Micah more questions and the room was there, but it was no office. It was empty. No desk, no furniture of any kind, and certainly no Micah."

"He was probably trying to reach you like he did me. Whatever is going to happen, Raven, he says you're important."

Raven's bottom lip folded under, and her hands ran down her skirt again. "I also had a flashback last night. At least I think it was a memory. I was pretty young, but I was at the park with my dad, and he told me they named me Raven because I would be a guide and lead people to the light."

"I believe that's exactly what you'll do," Kat said. "When the believers are raptured, there will be people with questions - people left behind who won't understand why they weren't taken, people who have never heard of the rapture and won't understand what happened, and people who denied God's existence and will still have trouble believing. The Bible said that many will come to know

God during the Tribulation. I think you will be integral in leading them to God."

"But why me? I don't even believe in God, not anymore."

Kat smiled. "I had lost my way too when Stella died, but God has his reasons. Sometimes, He chooses the least likely to demonstrate His power and glory."

Raven leaned back and her right hand lifted to her lips. Her index finger traced a slow pattern across her bottom lip. "You don't know me; you don't know what happened to me. I can't be anyone's guide. My life is too messed up."

Kat crossed to sit next to Raven. "You're right. I don't know your story, but I'm here to listen if you want to talk. What I do know is that God makes masterpieces out of messes, and He can use you. Besides, if I'm right about this, your story will soon become one of saving a lot of people instead of whatever happened in your past."

"What do I need to do?"

❦ 13 ❦

SUNDAY MORNING

"**H**ow long are we going to be stuck here?" Dave asked as he paced the small hotel room.

After picking Dave up from work the night before, they had driven to a local hotel and checked in. The truth was that Jordan had no idea what to do next. She was waiting for word from Jeremy, but his cell phone kept going to voicemail.

"I don't know, but Jeremy should be back soon." She hoped.

"Jeremy, the angel?" Disbelief oozed from Dave's words, but Jordan couldn't blame him. He hadn't seen Jeremy or whatever he had been fighting. Neither had Heather, but at least she had heard the commotion. She'd been a trooper, never questioning Jordan as they left her house behind. Now, she sat rocking Samuel softly on her lap, but her eyes were focused on the conversation going on between Dave and Jordan.

"Yes, the angel." Jordan sighed and checked her phone again. "Look, I don't know what else to tell you. I had visions of some dark shape over Samuel. Jeremy told me it was a demon, and when I grabbed Samuel, Jeremy was certainly battling something. Now, I don't know about you, but I'd like to make sure the house is safe, that Samuel is safe, before we go back there."

A knock sounded at the door, and Jordan pressed her eye to the spy hole before opening the door. Jeremy leaned against the frame on the other side, a weary expression on his handsome face.

"Are you okay?" Jordan asked, extending a hand to help him in.

"I will be. That demon was strong, but thankfully he was alone. For now."

"Are you Jeremy? Will you please explain to me what is going on?" Dave's voice thundered from behind them as Jordan shut the door.

"I will explain all that I can," Jeremy said as he sank onto the desk chair. He took a few deep breaths before sitting up straighter. "There is a war going on around you. It has always been there, but it is getting much worse now that the end is coming near."

"The end?" Heather whispered. It was the first thing she had said in hours.

"The end of this world. Soon, the believers will be raptured, and seven years of tribulation will befall the earth and those who are left upon it. The antichrist will rise and rule for a time before Jesus returns to send him and all his minions to the lake of eternal fire. Then God will create a new earth."

His words appeared to have a sobering effect on Dave as his next statement was calm. "So, this rapture will happen soon?"

Jeremy nodded. "I do not know the exact time. None of us do, but I believe it is close due to the increased demonic activity. Jordan here was chosen by God to receive visions and pass on what she sees in order to save people. The demons are aware of that and wanted to harm Samuel to make her less effective."

"But it's safe now, right? We can go home?" Heather asked in a small voice.

"Nowhere is truly safe, but I will stay with you as long as I can," Jeremy said.

"What about me?" Jordan was glad to know that Samuel was safe, at least for now, but how did that affect her mission?

"You should stay too," Heather said. "If there isn't much longer, you should spend the time you can with your son."

It was what Jordan wanted, but it felt selfish. She turned to Jeremy for his thoughts, but she could read his answer in his eyes. There was no need for her to return to the battlefield. The time was close.

"You'll fail, you know that right?"

Raven turned to see who had spoken to her, but it was too dark. There were only shadows.

"You are too damaged, too used up."

This voice came from behind her, but she could see no one there either.

"Who are you? What do you want with me?"

"We only want to tell you the truth." This time the voice came from her left, but the room was hopelessly dark. Raven could barely see her hand in front of her face.

Then a footfall sounded. And another. Raven's heart pounded in her chest, but she seemed incapable of moving, as if vines had sprouted from the floorboards and held her feet firmly in place.

"You are nothing. You've always been nothing."

No, she knew that voice, but it couldn't be. He was dead. She'd watched him die.

"Nothing but a few minutes of fun anyway." As the face of her stepfather appeared out of the darkness, Raven screamed.

She was still screaming when her eyes opened to reveal her bedroom. A dream. It was just a dream, but her heartbeat would not slow down. Nor could she seem to warm up.

And then a slow, eerie chuckle filled the room. "You can't do what she says. You are nothing. You will always be nothing. Useless. Garbage."

Raven's head whipped to the side, and another scream escaped as she spied the dark shape on the side of her bed. She threw back the covers and launched herself out of bed.

"No one will believe you. Crazy, they'll say." Another shape sat by her window.

She was going crazy. There had never been more than one shape. What did this mean? She turned to her closet to grab clothes, but suddenly the shapes were moving toward her. They would soon block her escape, so she pivoted and raced out of the bedroom. Grabbing her coat and purse, she paused only a moment before throwing open the front door. As she did, bright light filled the space behind her. She had no idea what that meant, but at the moment, she didn't care and she didn't dare look back.

Kat sat next to Patrick and tried to listen to the sermon, but her mind was miles away. She'd told Raven as much as she could about what to expect last night, but while the girl had listened, she had left with skepticism written all over her face. Not that Kat could blame her; it was a lot to take in. The problem was she had no idea what to do next, and she could feel that the end was coming soon.

"You okay?" Patrick whispered, leaning close to her.

"I don't know." There was so much she felt she still needed to do. She needed to finish the document she had started to leave for Raven. Even though she had told her everything on it, she knew the girl would probably not remember everything when the time came, so she needed to finish it and tell Raven where to find it. Plus, there were all the people she still hadn't reached. Their fate weighed on her as well.

"Okay, we'll head out as soon as it's over."

Kat nodded, but it didn't feel soon enough. "I'll be right back." She needed air and a break. Even in church where there should be no lights, she saw them. Not as much as outside, but still too many. Too many people who thought they were believers but hadn't truly given themselves over to God.

She pushed open the doors of the sanctuary and then exited the church. The sun was almost directly overhead sending warmth and light to the ground around her. Flowers were in bloom, and the grass was a vibrant green. She wondered if it would change after the rapture.

"Hello, Kat."

Micah. She turned to see him leaning against one of the columns.

"You've done well, Kat."

"I have? I feel like I haven't done anything. No one's light has left."

"You have planted seeds, left them with what they need to make their decision. That is all we asked of you."

"So, does this mean it's time?" Even though it shouldn't, the thought terrified her. This was all she'd known for decades, but it was all about to change.

He flashed a half smile. "Almost. I don't know the exact time, but all the events are in motion, and the demon activity is growing. It won't be long now."

"Will Raven be okay?"

"Her job will be difficult, but she will succeed, and you will see her again."

"And Jordan? Is she all right?" Kat hadn't heard from Jordan even though she'd left a message. She had planned to try her again today.

"She is. She saved her son, and Jeremy is protecting them for now."

"Jeremy? Her friend from the flight? How is he…" And then it hit her. "Jeremy is an angel too?"

Micah's smile radiated love and kindness. "There are angels all around. Our job is to guide and protect you. You were my charge. Jordan was Jeremy's."

"Does she know?"

He nodded. "She does now. I know you have questions, but I promise you they will be answered soon. You don't need to worry."

That was certainly easy for him to say, but he was an angel. He'd been to Heaven. He'd seen God. At least she thought he had. "What's going to happen to all of this?" she asked, waving a hand at the beauty around her.

His smile faded as his lips formed a tight line. "Before you return, this will all be destroyed, but what's coming will be better, Kat." He cocked his head as if listening to something she couldn't hear. "I have to go now, but I'll see you again."

And then he was gone before Kat could ask him any of the questions that had been weighing on her heart. With a sigh, she re-entered the church determined to spend whatever time she had left with Patrick and Maddie.

14

MONDAY AFTERNOON

Kat turned at the feel of a hand on her arm. Raven dropped her hand, but her eyes were wide with fear. "I need your help."

"What's going on?" Kat dropped her bag on a bench and motioned for Raven to sit, but Raven shook her head.

Her right hand rubbed up and down her left arm, and her eyes darted around the room before she spoke. "The dark shapes. They're getting worse. Yesterday, there were two in my room. I didn't even go home, just went straight to a hotel to spend the night. I can't take them much longer. They say things."

Kat nodded and placed a hand on Raven's arm. Though she had often heard the "things" Raven was talking about, she doubted she'd heard them in the same way, and she had certainly never seen dark shapes. She could only imagine how scary this was for Raven. "They're demons, Raven; it's what they do. Look, Micah came to see me at church yesterday. He said they are getting worse because the time is near. Now, I know what comes after won't be wine and roses either, but hopefully you'll get a reprieve."

Raven shook her head, her fierce bravado gone. "I don't think I can do this, Kat. What if I just accept God? I mean I've seen angels and demons so believing in God isn't that much of a stretch."

Kat's lips pulled into a sympathetic smile. If only it were that easy. "It's not enough just to believe He exists, Raven. Even the demons believe He exists. You have to accept Him as your savior and be willing to surrender your life to Him."

"Then I'll do that. I don't want to be left behind, Kat."

"Okay, I'll tell you how." Kat took a deep breath, but before she could say another word, she heard the sound of a trumpet. Bright light filled the area along with a feeling of absolute peace. She tilted her head to the light and felt herself rising into the air.

"Okay, I'll tell you how." Kat took a deep breath, but before she could say another word, the sound of screams grabbed Raven's attention. She raced out of the locker room to the scene of her dreams.

As if in slow motion, she saw the car burst through the front windows. Glass shattered in all directions - tiny shards spinning through the air. Faces froze in horror as the car barreled forward. Not a hand rose in protection, but the fear was etched on every face.

Where was the girl? In her dreams, there had been a girl in the way of the oncoming car. A girl she saved only to find nothing but clothes in her hand, but as she stood watching the scene unfold, Raven knew the girl was already gone. She had been taken at the same time the driver had. All the kids would be gone. And Kat. Kat would be gone as well.

"No." The word emerged as a primal scream, but no one seemed to notice. Even if they had heard her, they would have assumed she was screaming out of fear or anger. They would have no idea she was screaming because it was too late. She had waited too long to place her faith in God, and now she had been left behind like the other people in the gym. So many other people. Had nobody been taken besides Kat?

"Gemma? Has anyone seen Gemma?" A woman near the far wall held a shirt in her hands. Raven vaguely remembered seeing the woman as she walked in. She'd been entertaining a toddler with toys from the small stash Brian kept for younger siblings.

"Connor?" The shrill, high-pitched voice drowned out the other woman. "Connor, where are you?"

"Is everyone okay?" Brian rose from behind his desk where he must have been when the car hit.

"No, my son is missing."

"So is my daughter."

"Mine too."

Raven scanned the room. As bad as this was, it could have been a lot worse. Had it been six minutes later, people might have been killed, but it appeared no one had been in the path of the car. She glanced at the clock. It read 3:54. She waited for the hand to move, but it appeared frozen. 3:54. That's when it had happened. She wondered if there was any significance to the time. If Kat were around, she could have asked her, but Kat was gone. Raven knew without even returning to the locker room that she would find Kat's bag and her clothes, but the woman herself would be gone. Who would answer her questions now?

"Everyone spread out and look for the kids," Brian hollered.

Raven knew the kids would not be found. Maybe she would tell them, but they would think her crazy. Instead, she walked to the car. The driver - the same one from her dreams - looked up at her. Blood trickled down the side of his face from some cut, but he didn't seem concerned by it. "There was no one in the car. I swerved because it was coming right at me, but there was no one behind the wheel. How does a car drive with no one behind the wheel?"

But there had been someone. Until he or she was taken.

Raven wondered how many wrecks, how many crashes had just happened. How many people who had been left behind had been killed when the believers disappeared? Where did they go? They, like her, hadn't believed, but she had a chance to believe now and they didn't.

"Raven." Brian was shaking her shoulder. "Raven, are you hurt? Can you help look for the kids? They must have hidden somewhere when they heard the screams."

She turned to look at him. His voice still held a commanding note but also a trace of fear. Had he realized what had happened yet? "The children are gone."

"Gone? What are you talking about gone? They couldn't have just disappeared."

"They were raptured, Brian. Kat is gone too. All of them - those who truly believed - are gone."

She watched as the light of recognition dawned in his eyes, followed closely by fear, and then denial. "No, if the rapture had happened, I wouldn't be here. I believe in God."

"Even the demons believe in God, but to some He will say, 'I never knew you.'" Raven felt the words come out of her mouth, but she had no idea where they were coming from. "Matthew 7:21 says: 'Not everyone who says to Me, 'Lord, Lord,' will enter the kingdom of heaven, but only he who does the will of My Father in heaven.'"

She blinked at Brian as the words left her head. Where in the world had they come from?

"But I do believe. I'd even started praying again."

Raven shook her head. "I saw an angel, Brian, and I still didn't believe enough to make a life change. Even though you pray, can you really tell me you are living the will of God?"

His mouth opened and closed like a fish, but he had no words. She knew he didn't. He turned and walked away from her, and then the shapes flew in. They poured in from the open window and hovered around the people in the gym.

Raven stepped back as they flew around her, but she no longer feared them. Somehow, though she had no idea how, she knew they could not hurt her. Perhaps she knew in the same way she had been able to recite a verse from a book of the Bible she had never read - someone was guiding her. Was it God? Micah? Kat?

As the shapes hovered around her friends, her heart ached. She might be safe from them, but she doubted everyone else was. What would they do? Would they simply sow seeds of doubt and grief? Could they physically harm people? And where were the angels? Were they here too only hidden from Raven's sight?

Though she knew in her heart that Kat was gone, Raven returned to the locker room. Kat's bag sat on the bench and a foot in front of it lay the clothes Kat had been wearing. From the pile, something glinted in the light.

Raven reached down and picked up the object. She

turned it over in her hand and felt the weight. Not the weight of the item itself, but the weight of responsibility. Jesus' responsibility back then and hers now.

"I left something for you at my house. There's a key under the mat." The words felt like a whisper in Raven's ear. She lifted her face to the ceiling expecting to see Kat smiling down on her, but nothing was there. With trembling fingers, she unclasped the necklace and fastened it around her own neck. Somehow, she doubted Kat would mind.

Though commotion still raged on around her, Raven knew she had other places she had to be - things she had to get working on. She threw her bag over her shoulder and walked out of the locker room.

Jordan opened her eyes as the bright light faded. She blinked a few times until the area around her came into focus. The colors surrounding her were more vivid than anything she'd experienced on Earth. They shimmered and danced as if alive. From somewhere, Jordan could hear the sound of music floating on the air.

"Oh my gosh, is this Heaven?" Jordan turned to see three people behind her. Heather and Dave she recognized, and their eyes were wide with wonder as they turned in a slow circle. The third man she didn't immediately recognize but she felt as if she knew him.

"I think so." The last thing Jordan remembered was crouching behind the couch with her hands over her ears as the intense banging and screeching of demons pounding the outside of Dave and Heather's house permeated the air. Then she'd seen the light and heard her voice being called. Jeremy had said it was safe to go, and so she'd gone. It appeared Heather and Dave had too, but where was Samuel? "Samuel? Where's Samuel?" Surely the demons hadn't gotten him. Heather had been holding him tightly when the light appeared.

"I'm Samuel."

Jordan turned to peer closer at the man she had not recognized.

"Samuel? But you can't be. You were just a baby," Heather said as she stepped closer to the man.

The man held his hands out as he shrugged. "I don't know."

Jordan knew he was telling the truth, and she felt just the tiniest twinge of sorrow that she had missed Samuel growing up, but it didn't last long. There was no room for sorrow here.

"Jordan? Jordan, is that you?"

Jordan turned to see Kat and two others running toward her. "Kat?" Jordan flung her arms around Kat. "I'm so happy to see you again."

"Me too."

When the hug ended, Jordan turned to Patrick and the woman beside him who had to be Maddie. She had grown just as Samuel had.

"So, this is it, huh?" Patrick asked as he looked around. "This is where we wait until the tribulation is over?"

"I think so," Jordan said. "Not a bad place to wait, I guess." Suddenly she remembered the link she and Kat shared. "Kat, did you reach Raven?"

Kat nodded. "I did. In fact, she was about to accept God as her savior before Jesus called us. I don't know what comes next for her, but I'm sure she'll be okay. She has to be, right?"

The End!

Want to find out what happens to Raven during the Tribulation? Look for the next book coming soon.

Thank you so much for reading *A Spark in Darkness*. I hope you enjoyed the story as I really enjoyed writing it. If you did, would you do me a favor? If you did, please leave a review. It really helps. It doesn't have to be long — just a few words to help other readers know what they're getting.

❦ 15 ❦

NOT READY TO SAY GOODBYE
YET?

Raven is important and there is much more to her story. Be sure to watch for the preorder for that book coming soon (as soon as I have a title).

But until that book, why not try another great series. This is my Sweet Billionaires series which starts out with The Billionaire's Secret. Originally a part of the Heartbeats series and titled A Father's Love, I updated it when the billionaire craze hit the stores. Still, I think you'll really enjoy it. My father not only cried but says it's his favorite book.

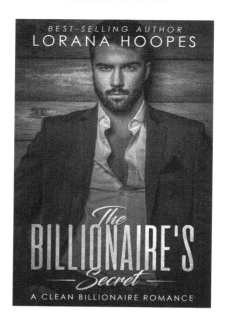

The Billionaire's Secret

He's a player who wants nothing but fun...

Until a blast from his past shows up on his doorstep with a little girl she claims is his daughter. Can Max be the father she needs?

Alyssa Miller has been tasked with making sure Peyton is okay...

But dealing with Maxwell Banks is harder than she thought it would be and her issues with trust aren't helping.

A misunderstanding ....

May ruin everything Max has been working so hard for.

Read on for a taste of The Billionaire's Secret....

THE BILLIONAIRE'S SECRET
PREVIEW

Maxwell Banks smiled at the buxom blond across from him. Her name had escaped his memory, but she would make a suitable companion for the night. The image of her long blond hair splayed like gold across his pillow filled his mind, sending his pulse into overdrive. Her yoga instructor body was just calling out for his attention if the tight shirt she was sporting was any indication.

Discreetly, he turned his wrist to check his watch. Fifteen minutes since they finished dinner. Surely that was a long enough segment of small talk. "You want to finish this somewhere more comfortable?" He reached across the table to stroke her hand as he said the words. A little flattery went a long way. He had mastered that art in the last few years.

Her tongue darted out and swiped across her lips, and her teeth bit the bottom one, causing the blood to flow to it and tint it a shade darker. "Um, sure, I guess that would be okay."

Her words were hesitant, and Maxwell knew he would have to turn up his charm. He didn't usually have to work hard to get women to come home with him. With his dark hair, blue eyes, broad shoulders, and chiseled chest his looks alone attracted many. The fact that he came from money attracted the rest. Those were the harder ones to get rid of, the ones after his money. They tended to show up uninvited and blow his phone up all hours of the day.

But this one wasn't looking for a sugar daddy. This one he picked up in yoga class. Yoga was not usually his thing; he preferred lifting and running, but his friend Justin had dared him to try the class, and as the instructor was hot, Maxwell had taken the chance.

He could tell when he entered the large room that she found him attractive as her eyes followed him as he crossed the room to grab a mat. His blue cut-off t-shirt had showed off his muscular arms and brought out his eyes, and his playing dumb had kept her by his side most of the class. Asking for her number had been easy after that. He had simply put on his puppy dog face and emphasized the need for private lessons if he was ever going to improve. She had fallen for it; hook, line, and sinker. Now it was time to seal the deal.

"Great." He whipped out his wallet and placed four twenties on the table. It was more than enough money as she only had salad and water–another perk to taking out weight conscious women. Then he stretched out his hand to her.

"Don't you need to wait for the change?" she asked, glancing around for the waiter.

"No, I believe in big tips." He flashed his best smile, hoping it would soothe some of the hesitation in her voice.

She shook her head in disbelief, but accepted his outstretched hand. He gave it a squeeze for good measure and then led her out of the restaurant and back to his black BMW Z4.

"What about my car? Shouldn't I just follow you?" She glanced around for her car in the full parking lot.

"Don't worry about it. I'll bring you back to your car later." Her smile relaxed as he opened the car door for her, and she slid into the grey leather seat.

After shutting her door, Max walked to the driver's side, folded himself into the driver's seat and turned on the engine. As the air had cooled considerably, he pressed the button for the heated seats before pulling out of the restaurant parking lot.

The girl—he really should remember her name— pulled on her skirt to stretch it back down. It had crept up her leg revealing her smooth, toned thighs underneath.

"Can I turn on some music?"

Max mentally kicked himself. He'd been so distracted with her thighs that he hadn't realized they were driving in silence. Silence was never good. It let them think. "Of course, whatever you'd like."

She punched the buttons on the dial a few times before landing on some newer pop music. Inwardly, he cringed–he was more of a hard rock fan himself, but he knew the payout would be worth it.

Fifteen minutes later, he heard the sharp intake of her breath as he pulled into the driveway of his house. While not a mansion, the 4000-foot ranch home was impressive. The craftsman style boasted three slanted roofs, two chimneys, a grey-brick exterior, and a white wraparound front porch. A small working fountain sat in the middle of the circular drive.

"You live here?" The awe was plain in her voice.

He smiled inside. The deal was almost sealed now. "Yeah, it's a little big for one person, but I hope one day to fill it with a family."

When she turned back to him, he could almost see the stars in her eyes.

He pulled into the three-car garage and parked next to his Harley Davidson. The third bay contained no vehicle. At least not yet. The garage was neat as Max detested messes, and the few tools he owned meticulously lined the shelves along the wall.

Her heels clicked across the cement floor as he led her

to the door into the house. It opened onto a large laundry room with a washer, dryer, and table to fold clothes on. The door from the laundry room led into the hallway. To the left was the kitchen, dining room, and family room. To the right were the bedrooms. Max turned left, leading her to where he had a bottle of wine waiting on the counter. It was yet another tactic he had learned would loosen women up and lower their inhibitions.

The large kitchen was half the size of the first floor of most houses. Stainless steel appliances filled the room, and a marble topped island in a crème color with brown and gold flecks sat predominantly in the middle of the room. A large silver light fixture hung above the island, and a deep sink took up a portion of the space under the light. The island hosted a bottle of red wine and two glasses, and across from the sink four plush barstools covered in black leather lined the island. The cabinets that circled the room were a deep brown, and a large walk-in pantry covered most of the back wall, but it was the wine Max focused on.

"Drink?" he asked as he uncorked the bottle and began pouring the glasses.

"Oh, I don't know if I should. I can't stay too long. I teach an early class tomorrow." The hesitation was creeping back into her voice, and her eyes darted around as if she might bolt. It was time to turn up the charm.

Max pushed his lower lip out in a slight pout. "You

wouldn't make me drink alone, would you? Besides, what will one glass hurt?" The glass he extended to her was half full, and he focused his steely blue eyes on her. Many women had told him that his eyes were what drew them in, and Max knew how to use them to his advantage.

Her eyes flickered back and forth, but returned to his gaze, and he knew he had her. "Okay, maybe just one." Her arm rose and accepted the glass.

"To a wonderful night with a beautiful woman," he said, clinking her glass ever so slightly. A blush spread across her face, and she dropped her eyes to the murky red liquid as she took a sip. Max was about to suggest they retire to the living room, where his leather couch would be more inviting and conducive to his seduction, when the doorbell rang.

A glance at his watch revealed it was nearly ten p.m. No one he knew should be ringing his bell, and it was too late for solicitors. "Make yourself comfortable," he said to her, "I'll be right back."

As his shoes echoed on the hardwood flooring, he cursed the timing of whoever stood on the other side of the door. He had worked hard to get this woman here, and she had proven more skittish than many before her. If he lost her because of this interruption, there would be retribution.

Max was fully prepared to lash into the unfortunate soul on the other side of the door, but when he swung it open, his heart stopped, and his words failed him. The anger sizzled as if doused like a campfire, and he blinked not believing his eyes.

Keep reading The Billionaire's Secret...

Or get all 4 billionaire books and save nearly 40%

❦ 17 ❦

A FREE STORY FOR YOU

Enjoyed this story? Not ready to quit reading yet? If you sign up for my newsletter, you will receive The Billionaire's Impromptu Bet right away as my thank you gift for choosing to hang out with me.

The Billionaire's Impromptu Bet

A SWAT officer. A bored billionaire heiress. A bet that could change everything....

Read on for a taste of The Billionaire's Impromptu Bet....

THE BILLIONAIRE'S IMPROMPTU
BET PREVIEW

B rie Carter fell back spread eagle on her queen-
sized canopy bed sending her blonde hair
fanning out behind her. With a large sigh, she
uttered, "I'm bored."

"How can you be bored? You have like millions of
dollars." Her friend, Ariel, plopped down in a seated position on the bed beside her and flicked her raven hair off her
shoulder. "You want to go shopping? I hear Tiffany's is
having a special right now."

Brie rolled her eyes. Shopping? Where was the excite-
ment in that? With her three platinum cards, she could go
shopping whenever she wanted. "No, I'm bored with shopping too. I have everything. I want to do something exciting. Something we don't normally do."

Brie enjoyed being rich. She loved the unlimited credit

cards at her disposal, the constant apparel of new clothes, and of course the penthouse apartment her father paid for, but lately, she longed for something more fulfilling.

Ariel's hazel eyes widened. "I know. There's a new bar down on Franklin Street. Why don't we go play a little game?"

Brie sat up, intrigued at the secrecy and the twinkle in Ariel's eyes. "What kind of game?"

"A betting game. You let me pick out any man in the place. Then you try to get him to propose to you."

Brie wrinkled her nose. "But I don't want to get married." She loved her freedom and didn't want to share her penthouse with anyone, especially some man.

"You don't marry him, silly. You just get him to propose."

Brie bit her lip as she thought. It had been awhile since her last relationship and having a man dote on her for a month might be interesting, but.... "I don't know. It doesn't seem very nice."

"How about I sweeten the pot? If you win, I'll set you up on a date with my brother."

Brie cocked her head. Was she serious? The only thing Brie couldn't seem to buy in the world was the affection of Ariel's very handsome, very wealthy, brother. He was a movie star, just the kind of person Brie could consider marrying in the future. She'd had a crush on him as long as she and Ariel had been friends, but he'd always seen her as just that, his little sister's friend. "I thought you didn't want me dating your brother."

"I don't." Ariel shrugged. "But he's between girlfriends right now, and I know you've wanted it for ages. If you win this bet, I'll set you up. I can't guarantee any more than one date though. The rest will be up to you."

Brie wasn't worried about that. Charm she possessed in abundance. She simply needed some alone time with him, and she was certain she'd be able to convince him they were meant to be together. "All right. You've got a deal."

Ariel smiled. "Perfect. Let's get you changed then and see who the lucky man will be.

A tiny tug pulled on Brie's heart that this still wasn't right, but she dismissed it. This was simply a means to an end, and he'd never have to know.

Jesse Calhoun relaxed as the rhythmic thudding of the speed bag reached his ears. Though he loved his job, it was stressful being the SWAT sniper. He hated having to take human lives and today had been especially rough. The team had been called out to a drug bust, and Jesse was forced to return fire at three hostiles. He didn't care that they fired at his team and himself first. Taking a life was always hard, and every one of them haunted his dreams.

"You gonna bust that one too?" His co-worker Brendan

appeared by his side. Brendan was the opposite of Jesse in nearly every way. Where Jesse's hair was a dark copper, Brendan's was nearly black. Jesse sported paler skin and a dusting of freckles across his nose, but Brendan's skin was naturally dark and freckle free.

Jesse flashed a crooked grin, but kept his eyes on the small, swinging black bag. The speed bag was his way to release, but a few times he had started hitting while still too keyed up and he had ruptured the bag. Okay, five times, but who was counting really? Besides, it was a better way to calm his nerves than other things he could choose. Drinking, fights, gambling, women.

"Nah, I think this one will last a little longer." His shoulders began to burn, and he gave the bag another few punches for good measure before dropping his arms and letting it swing to a stop. "See? It lives to be hit at least another day." Every once in a while, Jesse missed training the way he used to. Before he joined the force, he had been an amateur boxer, on his way to being a pro, but a shoulder injury had delayed his training and forced him to consider something else. It had eventually healed, but by then he had lost his edge.

"Hey, why don't you come drink with us?" Brendan clapped a hand on Jesse's shoulder as they headed into the locker room.

"You know I don't drink." Jesse often felt like the outsider of the team. While half of the six-man team was married, the other half found solace in empty bottles and meaningless relationships. Jesse understood that — their job was such that they never knew if they would come home night after night — but he still couldn't partake.

Brendan opened his locker and pulled out a clean shirt. He peeled off his current one and added deodorant before tugging on the new one. "You don't have to drink. Look, I won't drink either. Just come and hang out with us. You have no one waiting for you at home."

That wasn't entirely true. Jesse had Bugsy, his Boston Terrier, but he understood Brendan's point. Most days, Jesse went home, fed Bugsy, made dinner, and fell asleep watching TV on the couch. It wasn't much of a life. "All right, I'll go, but I'm not drinking."

Brendan's lips pulled back to reveal his perfectly white teeth. He bragged about them, but Jesse knew they were veneers. "That's the spirit. Hurry up and change. We don't want to leave the rest of the team waiting."

"Is everyone coming?" Jesse pulled out his shower necessities. Brendan might feel comfortable going out with just a new application of deodorant, but Jesse needed to wash more than just dirt and sweat off. He needed to wash the sound of the bullets and the sight of lifeless bodies from his mind.

"Yeah, Pat's wife is pregnant again and demanding some crazy food concoctions. Pat agreed to pick them up if she let him have an hour. Cam and Jared's wives are having a girls' night, so the whole gang can be together. It will be nice to hang out when we aren't worried about being shot at."

"Fine. Give me ten minutes. Unlike you, I like to clean up before I go out."

Brendan smirked. "I've never had any complaints. Besides, do you know how long it takes me to get my hair like this?"

Jesse shook his head as he walked into the shower, but he knew it was true. Brendan had rugged good looks and muscles to match. He rarely had a hard time finding a woman. Jesse on the other hand hadn't dated anyone in the last few months. It wasn't that he hadn't been looking, but he was quieter than his teammates. And he wasn't looking for right now. He was looking for forever. He just hadn't found it yet.

Click here to continue reading The Billionaire's Impromptu Bet.

THE STORY DOESN'T END!

You've met a few people and fallen in love....

I bet you're wondering how you can meet everyone else.

Star Lake Series:

When Love Returns: Can Presley and Brandon forget past hurts or will their stubborn natures keep them apart forever?

Once Upon a Star: Now that Blake has gained confidence and some muscle, will he finally be able to reveal his feelings to Audrey?

Love Conquers All: Now that Azarius has another chance with Laney, will he find the courage to share his life with her? Or will his emotional walls create a barrier that will leave him alone once more?

The Heartbeats Series:

Where It All Began: Will Sandra tell Henry her darkest secret? And will she ever be able to forgive herself and find healing? Find out in this emotional love story.

The Power of Prayer: Who will Callie choose and how will her choice affect the rest of her life? Find out in this touching novel.

When Hearts Collide: Amanda captivates his heart, but can Jared save her from making the biggest mistake of her life? A must read for mothers and daughters.

A Past Forgiven: Can Chad leave his bad-boy image behind and step up and be there for Jess and the baby?

Sweet Billionaires Series:

The Billionaire's Secret: Can Max really change his philandering ways? Or will one mistake seal his fate forever?

A Brush with a Billionaire: Will Brent and Sam's stubborn natures keep them apart or can a small town festival bring them together?

The Billionaire's Christmas Miracle: Drew Devonshire is captivated by the woman he meets at a masquerade ball, but who is she?

The Billionaire's Cowboy Groom: When Carrie returns to town requesting a divorce, can he convince her they belong together?

The Cowboy Billionaire: Coming Soon!

The Lawkeeper Series:

Lawfully Matched: Will Jesse find his fiancee's

killer? And when Kate flies into his life, will he be able to put his painful past behind him in order to love again?

Lawfully Justified: Can Emma offer William a reason to stay? Can William find a way to heal from his broken past to start a future with Emma? Or will a haunting secret take away all the possibilities of this budding romance?

The Scarlet Wedding: William and Emma are planning their wedding, but an outbreak and a return from his past force them to change their plans. Is a happily ever after still in their future?

Lawfully Redeemed: Dani Higgins is a K9 cop looking to make a name for herself, but she finds herself at the mercy of a stranger after an accident. Calvin Phillips just wanted to help his brother, but somehow he ended up in the middle of a police investigation and caring for the woman trying to bring his brother in.

The Still Small Voice Series:

The Still Small Voice: Will Kat be able to give up control and do what God is asking of her?

A Spark in the Darkness coming soon!

Blushing Brides Series:

The Cowboy's Reality Bride: Laney Swann has been running from her past for years, but it takes meeting a man on a reality dating show to make her see there's no need to run.

The Reality Bride's Baby: Laney wants nothing more

than a baby, but when she starts feeling dizzy is it pregnancy or something more serious?

The Producer's Unlikely Bride: Ava McDermott is waiting for the perfect love, but after agreeing to a fake relationship with Justin, she finds herself falling for real.

Ava's Blessing in Disguise: Five years after marriage, Ava faces a mysterious illness that threatens to ruin her career. Will she find out what it is?

The Soldier's Steadfast Bride: coming soon

The Men of Fire Beach

Fire Games: Cassidy returns home from Who Wants to Marry a Cowboy to find obsessive letters from a fan. The cop assigned to help her wants to get back to his case, but what she sees at a fire may just be the key he's looking for.

Lost Memories and New Beginnings: She has no idea who she is. He's the doctor caring for her. When her past collides with his present, can he keep her safe?

When Questions Abound A companion story to Lost Memories, this book tells the story from Detective Jordan Graves's point of view.

Never Forget the Past

Secrets and Suspense coming soon!

Stand Alones:

Love Renewed: This books is part of the multi author second chance series. When fate reunites high school sweethearts separated by life's choices, can they find a second chance at love at a snowy lodge amid a little mystery?

Her children's early reader chapter book series:
The Wishing Stone #1: Dangerous Dinosaur
The Wishing Stone #2: Dragon Dilemma
The Wishing Stone #3: Mesmerizing Mermaids
The Wishing Stone #4: Pyramid Puzzle
The Wishing Stone Inspirations 1: Mary's Miracle
To see a list of all her books

authorloranahoopes.com
loranahoopes@gmail.com

DISCUSSION QUESTIONS

1. What was your favorite scene in the book? What made it your favorite?

2. Did you have a favorite line in the book? What do you think made it so memorable?

3. Who was your favorite character in the book and why?

4. Raven faced anger issues in the book. Do you think they were justified?

5. What do you think would be the hardest part about having a gift like Kat or Jordan?

6. What did you learn about God from reading this book?

7. How can you use that knowledge in your life from now on?

8. What lesson can you take away from this book?

9. What do you think would make the story even better?

ABOUT THE AUTHOR

Lorana Hoopes is an inspirational author originally from Texas but now living in the PNW with her husband and three children. When not writing, she can be seen kick-boxing at the gym, singing, or acting on stage. One day, she hopes to retire from teaching and write full time.

Made in the USA
Middletown, DE
01 November 2022